PSYCHICS, MEDIUMS AND LIGHTWORKES YOU CAN FULLY TRUST!

Their names, specialties, services, how much they charge, and how to reach them.

Published in the United States of America.
Date of Publication: January 22, 2014
Printed by Times Square Press, New York and Berlin.

Author's website: www.maximilliendelafayettebibliography.org/biblio
Maximillien de Lafayette books are available at Barnes&Noble, amazon, and worldwide in paperback and at amazonin kindle edition.
For fast delivery, order your paperback edition at www.lulu.com
Contact: delafayette6@aol.com

PSYCHICS, MEDIUMS AND LIGHTWORKES YOU CAN FULLY TRUST!

Their names, specialties, services, how much they charge, and how to reach them.

Maximillien de Lafayette

TIMES SQUARE PRESS
New York

Table of Contents

Profile of the
The American Federation of Certified Psychics and Mediums Incorporated, New York...187

*** *** ***

Prologue

"Fully Trusted" means a lightworker who has demonstrated a high level of integrity, honesty and sincere commitment to clients.
However, it does not categorically mean that the lightworker in question is either the most successful/famous practitioner, or the best in the field.
Although, I have included in the book what I called "lightworkers you can fully trust", the expression "Fully trusted" does not categorically imply that I fully endorse all lightworkers' claims, personal philosophy and messages, especially in the context of highly debated topics and areas of practice.

There are numerous distinguished practitioners who made their mark on the landscape of the occult and in esoteric fields, and reach worldwide fame, yet, in some instances, were found to be deceptive and self-serving. Unfortunately that is the "nature of the beast"!
During my 50 years of involvement in spiritual matters, teaching, lecturing and authoring, I have met numerous psychics and mediums, healers and spiritual counselors, tarot readers and palmists, animal communicators and metaphysicians who were never mentioned in published works, who never appeared on television, or walked on the red carpet, yet, in my honest and professional opinion, they were/are the best, the most accomplished and the most "powerful" lightworkers of all time. Usually, enlightened teachers and practitioners are quite, and humble, and avoid pre-fabricated fame.
The present book refers you to lightworkers who are sine dubio, the most honest ones who genuinely care about you. And this is what really counts. "Fully trusted" also means a lightworker who has gained the respect and trust of clients. This trust and other forms of clients' gratitude are usually documented by public statements, recommendations and acknowledgement by satisfied clients, assuming that those statements, recommendations, and testimonials are real, bona fide, accurate, and not fabricated by lightworkers themselves, and who quite often, and unfortunately

use them as a tool and a propaganda medium to "catch" clients, and those who are in desperate need of spiritual guidance. It is a tough call!

There is no such thing as the "Perfect psychic", the "Perfect Medium", "Miracles' worker", "A divine messenger", a psychic who "Knows all the answers to your questions", a healer "Who cures all diseases", or a medium who "Commands angels, spirits and summons the spirit or soul of dead people in 50 seconds!!

Any lightworker who claims to be 100% accurate all the times IS delusional, for esoteric practices are not scientific, and the lightworker himself or herself is not the purest and the most powerful/enlightened living form in any dimension.

Only the Divine can claim such power! And lightworkers are not the incarnation of the Divine.

Lightworkers claims of "100% success" are unrealistic. There is no guarantee, whatsoever, that "perfect" results are obtained regularly, in any esoteric, metaphysical or spiritual endeavor (s).

And calling upon the soul of a departed one is not a "penny in the pocket" or a "Done deal" as often claimed by zillions of mediums.

Lady Patti Negri warned us against mediums exaggerated and false claims regarding this matter.

Meticulously I have reviewed the statements of the lightworkers mentioned in this book. And I took the liberty in discussing their abilities and their success ratio with all those who sent me letters of recommendations and personal testimonies attesting to their satisfaction.

I did it on purpose to satisfy my curiosity and to make sure that the clients' statements were genuine and not crafted and sent by lightworkers and/or their associates.

My investigations and "fishing expeditions" brought peace to my mind. I am confident that the lightworkers who are featured in the book are honest, loving, caring and truthful to the best of their ability.

*** *** ***

PART I
CANDID INTERVIEW WITH AMERICA'S BEST LIGHTWORKERS

PART I
CANDID INTERVIEW WITH THE MOST TRUSTED LIGHTWORKERS

Should we take the word and revelations of a lightworker for granted?
What guarantee do we have? And how about this mesmerizing and incomprehensible phenomenon of spirits' communication?
How do lightworkers communicate with the invisible world?
Who live there? How lightworkers talk to spirits? By the power of mind?
Telepathically? Spiritually?
Is there a particular esoteric protocol for contacting the spirits?
Another paramount question preoccupies our curiosity and our urgent quest for probing the unknown and learning about what the future or other dimensions are hiding from us? A question which is directly linked to the readiness of lightworkers when it comes to their disposition and readiness to provide a psyching reading? Is psychic reading a spontaneous process or does it require compliance with a spiritual protocol which necessitates preparation and harmonious esoteric synchronization with the rhythm of the invisible world?

Who can answer these questions?
Obviously the lightworkers themselves.
But can we ask any lightworker to provide adequate and honest answers?
Of course not. Only those who are blessed with genuine gifts are honestly capable to elucidate the matter.
Thus, we asked some of the most trusted, sincere, and effective lightworkers to share with us their opinions on the subject.

*** *** ***

15

Why should we trust psychics?

Suzanne Grace: The majority of psychics can be trusted; just like the rest of society, there are a few who may not behave in a manner that is acceptable but for the most part we are just like everyone else.

In fact, personally I hold myself to higher standards because of the information I receive and deliver.

What I say can change someone's life; therefore, what I say must be said very carefully. Psychics that have been tested have been validated by outside sources.

Their personal and professional lives are investigated to ensure that they uphold values as well as possess characteristics that are above reproach. That does not mean we do not get parking or speeding tickets just like everyone else, but I do make sure that I treat others with respect, do my best to pay my bills on time, do not gossip about others and lead a life lived with integrity.

If you can validate a psychic - he or she was referred by a trusted friend or relative, or you utilize a source (such as the American Federation of Psychics, Mediums & Healers or ESPsychics.com) you are ensured that the person you are hiring is trustworthy and does indeed have a gift that they can share with you.

Corbie Mitleid: Ah, the actual question is not "should" but "Why can we trust psychics?" If you get the right psychic -- one who understands that what they say, how they act can truly influence a person's life for good or ill -- you are getting someone who accepts personal responsibility for honesty, authenticity, and service.

The best psychics always have your best interests at heart. That does not mean that they will twist or soften information if there is a challenge ahead, but they will be able to say "Here are your opportunities and how to go after them; here are your challenges and how to work within them or get past/around them...here is your tool box for a wonderful life!"

To be chosen by Spirit to be a Lightworker is no small thing. And those of good repute who accept their "draft notice from God" have dedicated their lives to be trustworthy counselors.

Jennifer Wallens: I believe trust can only be earned over time by the accurate results given by a reputable psychic.

I do not believe the public should generally trust anyone that says they are a psychic, but they should do their homework, due diligence, first to look at the particular Psychic's reviews, credentials, and of course their personal website. Search for the Best Psychics and Mediums and other Light workers by using reputable sites such as ESPsychics and Best Psychic Directory, and unbiased organizations who compile the best in each category, such as the recent voting organized by Times Square Press for the Best of 2013-2014 as voted by the public.

Trusting and using your own intuition will help you to choose a good psychic or medium that will be compatible with your own energy as well. Remember that it is up to you to decide what information resonates with you, if it doesn't then discard it; you have free will and need to use your own Intuition as the final say on any matter.

Chinhee Park: We should trust psychics because we exercise our abilities on a daily basis and have an objective insight to someone else's life.

We are out to help heal people, help guide them with their life path and teach them about their own psychic abilities or gifts. We can get to the root of an issue, whether it be a past or present one, which will help the person to get in touch with their issues and deal with them to live a better life.

A person should use their own intuition and feel which psychic would benefit them and who they connect with when choosing a psychic. This ensures a positive and healing experience. We are here to help people, not hurt them. So, please use your intuition and know that you don't have to pay hundreds and thousands of dollars to get a good, quality, loving psychic reading.

Melissa Stamps: Psychics' talent and ability to connect to dreams, unseen worlds, Spirits, heightened senses (The 5 CLAIRS); trance, events, and other energetic states is as ancient as dreaming. Psychics create a connection between the seen and unseen universes of experiences, feeling and being...I believe that everyone has the talent to have psychic experiences.

17

Some of the most intense turning points in my life came from working with Psychics. I was able to get crystal clarity on some incredibly important choices in my life that led to many new opportunities.

Trusting a psychic is trusting the person who is psychic. It is also trusting the intuitive, non-linear flow of feeling and connection to source. When people understand how many eons' people have gone to psychics for help, and how every ancient and modern culture has had psychics, there are a million awesome reasons to trust psychics!!!

Kimberly Ward: Trusting a Psychic is no different than trusting any other professional; your hairdresser, mechanic, babysitter, etc. Psychics are professionals that spend a great deal of time, energy and money to develop their skills just like any other professional.

I believe that everyone is intuitive in their own right and when you meet a psychic and have a reading with them you will know if you like them and can trust them. It is gut instinct. This is the same for any professional that you choose. If you go to a new hairdresser and have your hair done and do not like the haircut you do not go back, whereas, if you loved it, the hairdresser just made a client for life. It is the same with psychics.

In life we have to trust and have faith otherwise we would never move, never take chances and never receive the reward that taking risks offer.

My goal when working with a client is to help them find clarity on issues that have them confused so they can continue to move forward. Not shatter their world with promises they cannot yet see.

Sunhee Park: I believe that not all people will ever trust psychics because their soul is not supposed to be open in this lifetime. There are many people who get along great in this world being in denial and not wanting to learn about the unknown. They are content on living life based on tangible evidence, and facts.

People who are sensitives, and have a contract with the higher sources and god like powers such as aliens, angels, and spirit guides; are not whole if they do not learn about the unknown.

The unknown knowledge helps them fill the voids of past lives, present lives, and future. They are thirsty for the reason, rhythms and whys of all things they cannot touch. They can trust psychics that they feel a connection with, and they can tell the authenticity of who is channeling and who the real deal is.

It is an inner feeling, you can't explain it to someone who is not open to the unknown.

Patti Negri: Because psychics can be an amazing helpmate, resource and tool in one's life, development, happiness and self understanding! Yes, you have to make sure it is a real, honest and reputable psychic. That is why The American Federation of Certified Psychics and Mediums exists.

And one's own intuition and heart should also always be your main guide to picking a psychic. But a good psychic can truly help guide you through life's tough spots.

They can be a wonderful combination of confidant, spiritual advisor, friend and guide. We all need help along the way – and a good psychic or lightworker is often just the ticket to help you on your journey!

Robert Rodriguez: We should trust psychics because they have been given the gift of foresight and prophecy to help guide us when we need directions.

Although, one must be cautious of some whom chose to call themselves psychic, you can differentiate real from fake because a real psychic will always provide validation and will ask few questions.

Shannon Leischner: When I read this question I want to reword it to say, which psychic should be trusted? There are, just like in all things, good and bad psychics. We must look within ourselves and our instincts to feel which psychic best fits our needs. When intuition doesn't work, we can ask our friends and families for recommendations on the best psychic.

Another way to ensure that you are getting a psychic who cares about you and is truly skilled in what they do, is to look at organizations like ESPsychics and The American Federation of Certified Psychics and Mediums.

Organizations like these have tested and monitored their psychics and the feedback given by the people they read.

They hold the highest of standards when it comes to the psychics and healers that they choose to represent. In reality there are only a small number of psychics who are out to mislead you for a dollar.

For the most part, the intention of a psychic is to help give insight and facilitate healing. It is truly all about integrity and the innate desire to help that sets quality psychics apart from the rest.

There is a misconception that psychics work with dark energies and get messages from malevolent sources. Everything that I do is all about energy and service to my higher power who I choose to call God. Moreover, the psychics I work with and have had the ultimate pleasure of being associated are filled with love, light, and a true desire to be in service.

The people at ESPsychics and The American Federation of Certified Psychics and Mediums, are talented light workers, who truly care about people, and can be trusted to help.

Jethro Smith: I would have to say that one should not "trust psychics," one should trust rather the guidance in accordance with one's inner conscious. As a person who was "born with the gift" which heightened greatly after an experience around the age of five and a drowning experience where I was resuscitated at age eight, it is my belief that every person has "psychic ability" or "intuitive ability."

This ability becomes "heightened" or develops more strongly with various life events, traumas, training, and for numerous reasons which we do not yet understand. After my near-death-experience, to my surprise I could see and hear deceased persons who had crossed-over, and I could speak with "spirits on the other side" as well, who I referred to as angels.

As a youngster, I noticed that only some of my peers could simultaneously hear and see some of what I was experiencing.

In particular, for example, a handicapped young boy in kindergarten was also able to communicate; he seemed (to me) to have developed stronger metaphysical gifts to perhaps compensate for the physical handicap.

Later, when the handicap lessened thanks to medical science, the metaphysical gift he enjoyed decreased noticeably.

Later, I was trained by several metaphysical masters to enable me to understand and to develop aspects of my gift(s), sparing me much struggle and turmoil of "abilities and situations" I could not possibly have understood at such a young age. From this, it was clear to me that everyone is "psychic" at some level. I learned beyond a doubt that this ability can be either heightened or suppressed.

As each person is responsible for their individual life choices, so is each person responsible for how they seek information along the path of their life's journey: whether via books, universities, parents, or spiritual outlets such as church or counselors, or via the unique insight of a person such as a psychic or intuitive who can communicate with the spirit world, communicate with one's ancestors, and/or see "flashes" of significant events from the past or from the future.

Foresight becomes the gift of hindsight when one is enabled with a bit of foresight to adjust their choices, decisions, and emotions, especially during stressful times and times of great change.

Perhaps it is ironic that as an intuitive person familiar with using the sixth sense and as host of a talk-radio show called "Psychics Gone Wild," I would express any caveat of "trusting a psychic."

However, it is very clear to any professional psychic, intuitive, empathy, medium who has developed their sixth sense that there are many, many metaphysical gifts and levels of skill - hearing, seeing, feeling - not to mention interpreting what the spirit world portrays to the channel as a symbol or perhaps simply as a sound or a song.

Further, because this is a spiritual topic, one must always ensure that the psychic and the spirit is "in the light" and in accordance with one's spiritual beliefs. As a light worker, I feel that the assistance of a gifted light worker can be an enormous blessing in helping other people.

I strongly encourage even my own clients, however, and especially my students to make their own life choices - do not try to abdicate the responsibility to another by "trusting" anyone to make those determinations for you. The assistance of a gifted light worker / psychic can be invaluable.

April Ashbrook: In our work people have expressed a true concern of "fake psychics & Mediums". We have been given a bad reputation! But I have a true intention to look at the positive side of being a 'Real psychic'! It started when I went to LA for the conference back September 2013! I met such great light workers and knew I wanted to be a federation member! I believe in your mission to certify us as legit! This "membership will cool off" the skeptics and spirit takes care of the rest!!

John Cappello: Finding a reputable psychic may be the best investment a person can make to help them with issues. A good psychic should be trusted because they validate our situation in life and provide us with valuable insight. The perspective given by a psychic can make all the difference in the world when we are faced with a challenge that we are having difficulty in resolving.

When a psychic is on the energy path of a situation in our life they can startle us with their accuracy and the clarity they can give us.

The spiritual perspective of a psychic is non-judgmental and is only about the issue at hand. Often, the future resolution of a situation is predicted giving a client the "edge" or the closure they need to know is coming.

A trusted psychic is a valuable asset to take advantage of but even the best advice of the most reputable of psychics should be personally evaluated by the client. Ultimately, it is the client who should make the final decision in their life.

Dependency upon a psychic is not healthy but having more information and perspective is not only healthy but smart!

Van Doren Figueredo: I highly recommend people do their research before seeking a legitimate psychic and see what information is found behind their name. Not many trust psychics unless they have an excellent reputation or have been referred by word of mouth. Ask yourself the following questions before finding a real psychic.

Do they have a legal address? Phone number? Website?

Are they certified? Are there testimonials?

What is their reputation? Is any negative documentation found about the psychic anywhere?

There are very good psychics out there and a true psychic will not judge or tell you what you want to hear.

They speak from the heart and are honest and will never beat around the bush. Psychics validate what you already know and will want to help you and never challenge you or carry ego. It's not about power and true psychics will only speak truth!

If they just want your money, you're looking in the wrong places. It's about the quality not quantity. Trusted psychics are now being looked upon for their confidentiality, professionalism, ethics and integrity.

Chanda Reaves: A person should not trust in psychics but look within in ones self to obtain a spiritual intuitive answer, foremost. A psychic advisor should assist in giving confirmation to what the questioner intuitively has deducted through their own inner sense of knowingness through connecting with the divine source within themselves without giving hints, clues or any information.
Because of the lack of knowledge and practice of this important technique by clients, the psychic industry has become tainted by unprofessional-self proclaimed predatory psychics who abuse a clients "trust" or exploit the "lack of trust" within the client themselves to go within and feel the vibration of truth naturally, in which clients are taken advantage of, unfortunately.
I do not recommend becoming dependent nor co-dependent upon a psychic.
One must learn to enhance their own intuitive abilities when working with psychics and develop ones own gift of discernment so that one is able to discern whether the information that they are receiving is in fact reliable and/or resonates with "truth" from within. Truth in its self has its own vibration that can be "felt".
However, by doing the necessary due diligence of researching a psychics trustworthiness, accuracy, reliability are also factors that must be ascertained and thoroughly considered, whether one is psychically-spiritually in-tuned to oneself or not.

Dena Flanagan: To trust a psychic? hmmm, that is a subject close to my heart.
I sincerely believe you need to earn that trust when you are putting yourself out there to the world as a lightworkwer.
Psychics are the people who come to you through word of mouth, the people who come because someone has already had a reading by you and they liked it so much, so they referred you to someone else.
My advice is when you are looking for a psychic, make sure you know someone who has already been to this person and has a

good reputation within the community and with the people they have read.

The reason I say this is because there are people out there who are just trying to make a quick buck and genuinely don't care for your well being. Early on in my journey, I would test this out.

I have been to several psychics myself, kind of like a curious understudy and on that journey I did encounter psychics who would try to manipulate you into paying more by telling you there was a dark cloud or negative energy or a curse on you and for more money they will lift it.

So if anybody does this, please do not believe it. A good psychic would never do that and you should never have to pay more than agreed upon when you started. Do not let fear take you over, that is what they prey upon.

When you find a good psychic, yes for sure you can trust them.

A good psychic has your well being in mind and their main focus or goal is to just help you in a positive way so that you can move past your blockages and get on your true path.

Remember though that we all have free will and what you choose is up to you. Don't let anyone tell what you have to do; you make your own decisions based upon the information your guides are giving you. As a psychic who is trying to help, we will show you your choices but again the rest is up to you.

A psychic is there for clarity and for confirmation because life has a way of getting confusing and sometimes we all need that extra help for the clarity and hope so we may move on in life in a positive clear way.

You must always remember you are your own light and that we all have intuitive abilities, it is a matter of trusting that intuition.

Melissa Berman: I think that the term "Psychic" sometimes is misleading. I practice the healing arts which includes psychic work.

the right reader takes a little research, just like finding the right lawyer, physician and the like ~ one might try different readers on different occasions before finding that "go to" person. So many times a client is feeling vulnerable, hurting and seeking comfort and answers.

A good reader is going to provide to the best of her/his ability tools and answers to assist the client.

Sessions with me usually offer a little "homework" for the client. Discovering one's soul's mission and purpose is an ongoing process. A good reader contributes to the spiritual growth and empowerment of the client on the path.

*** *** ***

Communication with spirits, angels, deceased
people, and multi-dimensional entities.

Do you communicate with particular spirits or entities? Do you know who they are...names for instance? And are these spirits, angels, deceased people or something else?

Suzanne Grace: I personally communicate with the deceased loved one's of the person I am working with; I will also use my grandmother - who has passed as well - as a resource when I am unable to connect to someone's guides (people sometimes block us out of fear).

I also have guides - one has been identified as Moses; that's another story (unless you want to hear it!) but he is a great, loving resource to me and helps me when it comes to delivering information that has a religious basis to it as well as giving me a kick in the pants at times.

I also communicate with angels. I spent quite a long time learning about them as well as recognizing each angels energy when it is near. I have received information from one's guides who are Pleadian, but the information is very high level at times and can be difficult to understand.

However, when I channel, I do not need to know it, the client does and it always makes sense to them.

I have also communicated with the guides of my clients; sometimes these guides are Native American warriors or chiefs and the information is so beautiful. It gives us great insight to the client as well.

Corbie Mitleid: As a medium and a channel, I communicate with many discarnates (beings not in form at the moment). I have spoken with deceased loved ones who give minute details about our relationships that only they could know; it's clear who they are and they acknowledge when I get a name.

Spirit guides and angels will give their names, though often with amusement; names are not as important to them as they are to us! I know that my closest personal "guides" are beloved souls that I fought side by side with in World War I, and who still honor our bond.

My own angel, Baruchiel, comes in with channelings that often give me information or opinions that are definitely not mine -- but if I am being a "clear channel" I don't change what I'm getting, because the person with whom I'm sitting needs the information precisely as it's given.

Jennifer Wallens: During a mediumship reading, I am communicating with various and numerous spirit entities of deceased people that often give their names and evidential facts to prove they are who they say they are. Other times, I know my team of spirit guides who are deceased entities are giving me information for a particular client, and I am sometimes given names for guides that are working with a particular client; with what I believe are angels. These beautiful lights are of a higher vibration, which I can literally feel. Often I am in contact with a team of all sorts of Guides, I am not told whether or not they have been incarnate before usually, these entities are working as teams, they do not want individual praise or attention.

They may give us names to make us feel more comfortable, although it really isn't necessary as I feel the information, as long as it is helpful, is the most important part of the reading, not where it came from.

Chinhee Park: Yes, I do communicate with particular spirits or entities. I do know several spirit guides personally and a few I do not know personally and a few I don't know at all.

I do have some family members and friends who have passed. My mother, brother, grandparents, uncles, aunts and cousins are some of my guides.

Archangel Michael is another guide that appears a lot to help me. I also have an E.T. guide and some others I do not know who they are, I just feel they are there for me.

Melissa Stamps: Yes, I do communicate with specific Spirits, Guides and entities. I have a spirit guide named Francois who is/was a French film maker.

He works with me on my clairvoyance and how I see. He helps me see and process visual information and seeing close up and the bigger picture. He is brilliant demanding and emotional. I also work closely with a young French girl who was from 1930's. She says her name is Estelle and she comes from the stars. A lot of guides who feel like they come from other star systems bring through amazing symbols and information in my dreams.

They sometimes they appear in human form, but I can also feel their presence. They often do not give names. I dream journal though, so I have lots of amazing information from them. There are other Spirits and Guides that work with me on specific life issues like business and health. A beautiful actor friend of mine crossed over in the 1990's.

He helps me with teaching, workshops and being healthy and image stuff. There are many others as well. Sometimes I ask for assistance from Guides for the highest and best intention of what is needed in that moment.

Kimberly Ward: Yes, I communicate with many spirits I call them 'my committee'.

Some of my guides serve a specific purpose. Some are animals as well. I know many of their names, however, not all. They tell me that it is not needed to call upon them I only need to visualize their assistance. My grandfather is also a powerful guide for me and his passing launched me more fully into this work and he is very insistent that I help people. In life he taught me that no matter what your situation or status you always have something to give.

So this is what I do, it is my purpose. I also have many angels and work with some of the Arch Angels. Most of my guides have made their presence known during Shamanic Trance work. In addition to my grandfather being a primary driving force, I have a Native American guide who heads up my council of elders. I know his name, but most of the guides that walk with him offer assistance but he is the one I communicate with.

I also communicate with deceased loved ones of my clients when they have something to say. I find that most times it is when a client is struggling with the death of a loved one that they come forward to help the person through their grieving. I have a tremendous sense of humor and love to connect with spirits that also share the enjoyment of joy and humor.

I have even had cartoon characters show up that had tremendous meaning for my client.

Sunhee Park: Yes, I do communicate with aliens. As I have evolved in my practice as a psychic healer, my guides have changed. I used to have an Asian medicine man who would help me do energy healings. This past year I have a new guide that I know is an alien guide due to the vibrational difference and dimension. His name is Jeremiah, and he was a messenger of GOD and for the Jewish people. He was abused, slandered, and had near death experiences. People hated hearing the truth from him, but he kept spreading the word.

I can relate to him on a personal level, and I feel connected to his soul. People slander me, ridicule me, deny my gifts and I have had near death experiences, so I am very happy to have him as my alien guide. I also call in the Counsel to come help me when it comes to world or global events. I tap into the higher dimensions because I feel that my guides have expanded to the higher powers of "off worlders."

My goal is to keep practicing and exercising my gifts and channeling abilities to the highest.

Patti Negri: Yes, I often work with particular spirits and entities. Including deceased loved ones, beings from the angelic or star realms as well as spirit guides.

I also work with pure energy itself and tap into universal consciousness or ancestral memories and spirits that encompass pure information like the Akashic records or peoples bloodlines.

Robert Rodriguez: I personally do communicate with the deceased, people's spirit guides, guardians, ancestors, master teachers, and I at times have communicated with people's guardian angels, animals.

I am always aware of whom I am speaking and seeing because I constantly ask my guides to filter the spirit and also because I ask the spirit to tell me information that only the spirit and the person I am reading for would know. I am constantly asking for confirmations through out my readings so that the individual whom I'm reading for is assured we have contacted whom they've requested to contact. As far as getting names sometimes it's as simple as asking the spirit and the spirit telling me and at times I get sounds or letters, however, I do get names.

Shannon Leischner: I am a spirit communicator, which includes angels, guides, guardians, elemental energies, deceased loved ones, pet spirits, and all those who have a spirit, just like in life, I cannot guarantee who will communicate with me at any given time. I can usually tap into or communicate with just about any type of spirit.

I do, however, make sure that all my spirit communications are restricted to those who come in Gods light.

Communication with lower level, dark or malevolent energies, although possible, is not my thing. Each spirit has a particular energy signature, just like people, we are able to sense the energy of our mother or loved one next to us and can identify who they are without looking at them. It is a knowing and feeling. As all of us are made up of energy, different types of spirits vibrate at different rates of speed (called frequency). I have experienced that the closer the spirit is in relation to God, the higher the frequency of the spirit.

For instance, angels have a much higher frequency than a spirit of a deceased loved one. When communicating with spirits, I usually can quickly identify what type of spirit is making contact by their frequency and energy signature. Usually when I am approached or tap in to a loved one they will start to give me the pain of the ailment that they had when they were here or the pain of how they passed. An example of this is when I did a gallery reading in Los Angeles.

The night before the event, I dreamt about a man who was killed when his plane exploded while flying over a farm surrounded by jungle. While arriving at the event location, I started to have a ringing in my right ear (like the ringing one would have if they are near a very loud noise or explosion). As I was reading people at the event, the ringing in my ear got very intense and then I lost my hearing in my right ear.

I then mentioned my dream to the crowd and this lady raised her hand and said her brother was a pilot and died when his plane exploded over a farm in Cambodia.

After that I thought I would regain my hearing because the man had been identified, but it turned out that there were four more people at the event who had male loved ones who had died in some sort of explosion. If the spirit didn't have an ailment or pain when they passed, they will show me some characteristics that they possessed like appearance, mannerisms, and phrases they used. Amazing how spirit works.

Jethro Smith: Yes, I do speak with the spirits, as in I speak with my guides, one of whom is my grandfather. Since his passing, he has become my spiritual guide and before him, a Native American guide who I have called "Chief" since early childhood. In my experience, I have found that many people are guided at some level of their consciousness by loved ones who have crossed over.

Sometimes a client will "feel" the presence of a loved one, and it is a moving experience to provide validation of their presence and a confirmation of the ongoing love/connection between them as I relay the message of the deceased, as would a translator.

April Ashbrook: Who do I communicate with? I have Spirit Guides who tell me who I'm speaking to. I have boundaries made and written to help ask the spirits who they are. I channel Archangels, and ascended Masters, etc., and I know by the colors I see. My guides tell me they are Gabriel, Haniel, Uriel, Michael.

John Cappello: Yes, I communicate with particular spirits and entities. They are a range of spirits and entities communicating from different realms.
Loved ones, guides, angels, animals, elementals and extraterrestrial beings often communicate with me from other dimensions.
The most moving communications are from God. Each spirit and/or entity resonates a particular energy for me to sense.
They are all different and I can use my extended psychic senses to evaluate who they are and the information they want to communicate. I have learned to feel, see, hear, smell, taste and know when an entity is around me. It has taken years of practice to learn about the different types of energies that make contact with us and it continues to be a work in progress.
I never stop learning about those that exist, "beyond the physical," but I believe I have been called to work with them.
I have made this my life's work and they give me the information they want me to know.
I do hear names and know many of the spirits who are around me. Many spirits stay in my home with me and communicate they knew me in previous incarnations. It may not be their time to interact with me in the physical but they remain part of my soul group.
Some of them are relatives but I have many guides and angels around me as well. There are times when some entities come around to just visit. When I work with a client I am able to work with the entities around them whether they are loved ones, guides, angels, a beloved pet or others who may have something they desire to share.
It is a very fascinating experience that I communicate with working with a client. I learn so much about the soul journey of my client and of my own soul's quest.

The spirit world is a fascinating place to interact with if we just allow ourselves to be open it. I am privileged they trust me to communicate their insights.

Van Doren Figueredo: I do communicate with spirits and angels such as; Archangel Michael, Ariel and a few others. Every reading is extraordinary and not alike and I never really know what will take place during a mediumship reading. Sometimes they will be enlightening, give closure to a situation or even empower the client and/or myself. My most recent channeling was an ET elemental, a Kachina spirit and Orion which was a constellation. I will admit this is a very new experience. It taught me more about our existence here on earth.

One must have a very open mind and full of balance to be capable of connect with spirits. I will never allow to be used as a portal for any negative being or spirits, as this is not my forte. I am grateful to be a candidate in channeling spirits. If it was done in the past lifetimes I do believe nothing has changed today. Being a sensitive or intuitive 'psychic' we are just more advanced with the energetic connection.

Chanda Reaves: Throughout my life experience, I have had this fortunate opportunity to communicate with several types of spiritually Higher Lifeforms, Ascended Masters, Angelic beings, various Inter-dimensional beings, Extraterrestrials, Humans and Animal spirits, as well as Elementals. In addition, I have been in the presence and communication on many levels with Archangel Michael, Saint Germain, Kwan Yin, Biaviians, Pleiadians, Sirian Council, Arcturian Council, Nibiruan Council, Ishtar, Ashtar-Command and my African, Native and Irish Ancestors.

Dena Flanagan: I am a psychic, a medium and a healer and each one is very different. As a psychic, I have several spirit guides and these are the ones I communicate with.

I was born with the gifts of hearing, seeing, feeling and being able to talk to my spirit guides and I have had one that has been with me since I came to this earth; it is a man with an Irish brogue and then I have had another one since about the age of 25, it is a woman of an angelic realm and the two of them are my main helpers.

In the course of all the years I have been reading there have been ones that come in for short time periods to help me through whatever growth I was going through at the time and then they move on.

As a medium, I call directly in the people or person that the client wants to talk to. It is a whole different energy than talking with your spirit guides. It is more like channeling in that person and they are talking through you and you feel their stuff when they were alive and the stuff when they passed. It is like they are talking to you directly and they are only using my body as a tool to come through to bring you the messages.

As a healer, I call in archangels and angels and everybody who needs to come in to work on your body. I am able to see what is going on in your body as far as health issues, blockages and energy drains and the team of people that I can see, that come in to help are usually quite amazing and they use me as a vehicle to do the work that needs to be done, they show me where to go and what to do and they also talk to me.

Melissa Berman: I work with my Spirit Band which includes my guardian angel, master teacher and many other blessed beings. When in session, I have the client's permission to connect with her/his team. At that time, other blessed beings may come in such as ascended masters, animal spirits, faeries and all to share guidance with the client depending upon the client's needs at that time.

Everyone has the opportunity to connect with archangels, saints and all blessed beings as long as it is done with reverence, respect and gratitude. A client may have awareness of her/his team, but may need a little extra assistance in connecting ~ and that can come into a reading as actually meeting one's guides or even receiving ways to connect on one's own. In mediumship work, sometimes the client just needs a little validation that she/he is receiving messages from a loved one who has crossed over; and some sacred suggestions for connecting further can be provided during the session if that is the client's request.

*** *** ***

GETTING READY FOR PSYCHIC READING.

GETTING READY FOR PSYCHIC READING.

Do you prepare for your psychic reading, or is it a spontaneous process?
In other words, are you always ready to read for clients?

Suzanne Grace: I will do both; if I am meeting with a group of people or a one-on-one that is booked in advance, because of all of the energy, I will prepare by meditating, using crystals to protect myself as well as oils.

However, when I receive a phone call, I must be ready to go and as such I can deliver a spontaneous message to clients. I will ensure I am protected by performing protection prayers for the day and after each appointment or call, I will send back the energy.

Corbie Mitleid: Being a psychic and intuitive means one always keeps the engine in top shape, so to speak, so that as necessary you *can* drop into trance quickly. But one of my iron-clad rules is that I will not read anyone who does not sit with me or ask me to read them formally; no "drive by psychic shootings" in the grocery store from this intuitive! It's part of question #1 about trusting your psychic. If a perfect stranger walks up to you and starts giving you information in a public place that you are not ready for, how can you trust what you are given?

How do you know this person is the real thing?

My guides and angels understand that the courtesy of an "official request" means that I am being given the sacred trust of another soul to assist in their life, and that's when we all come to the conference table.

Jennifer Wallens: I used to sit for a few minutes and meditate, and say a prayer to connect, then wait until I could literally feel my guides present but after a year of doing that I realized I could just as easily connect instantly when I cleared my mind and focused on the client.

My guides are always ready and willing to help.

I remember when I was just starting out thinking I could never do instant readings such as on a phone service, but soon realized the information is always out there to connect with, intent is the key.

I do however, like to say a prayer to myself right before I start working for the day, asking God, Goddess, all this is to help me to connect and

give the information that will help my clients most.

I also meditate regularly for my own spiritual growth which I know only helps me as a Psychic and Medium, it is a crucial part of being a true spiritual light worker and in keeping myself in the right frame of mind and energy state.

Chinhee Park: I would have to say that I don't prepare for a reading, it's pretty much spontaneous. The only thing I do before a reading is make sure I'm clear headed, no noises, fully rested and feel good. If I feel somewhat off, sick, or not fully there emotionally to do a reading due to personal reasons or just not feeling up to par, I will re-schedule. I feel that I have to be at my best in order to be accurate and to give the best of my energies to someone.

Melissa Stamps: Both actually.

I love the sacredness of ceremony and creating energy that is mysterious to call in Spirit.

I work with casting Circles, meditation, mantras, pure sound, and breathing to get into a theta state. I also love in the moment readings. I was on a really long train ride. I was sitting next to a woman with several small children.

I looked at her and said, I see a man to your right, who is wearing a loose fitting jacket and a hat. He says he is a musician, and he is holding a saxophone. She said, that's my grandfather.

He was a musician who played the saxophone. He gave me a message for her that made gave her insight into to choice she had to make. It was totally unexpected. When clients call, and they want a reading right now...spontaneous readings are an awesome way to call on your Guides and higher self for fast downloads!!

Kimberly Ward: I use to believe that 'I had to prepare', this was head trash, a limiting belief. As soon as someone starts to talk, or as soon as I begin to read an email, the process starts; the visuals come in the message flows.

The only things that can interrupt this divine channeling is me and my head. I believe this is the largest struggle for anyone to block their intuition whether professional psychic or not. If I am doing Soul Retrieval work then preparation is a must.

I use the drum to induce a Shamanic Trance state to go back into the past of the client.

It is very deep work. For scheduled readings I always say a prayer and invite in both my own and any guides or deceased loved ones around my client that wish to be present. Everyone has free will including spirits.

Sunhee Park: I do have to prepare to do readings, because if I do it when I am preoccupied; its not fair to the client. They have to have my 100% focus and attention to their reading. I have to be in a quite place, and in a clear state of mind. I need at least 15 minutes to be ready for a reading, and an hour if they have deep and heavy drama. It is only fair that you are in a clear and quite space to give your best, but that is how I work.

I also cannot do reading after reading because information can mesh into the next reading from the last one. Thank you so much for giving me this opportunity to answer these questions.

I will always be grateful to express any words or wisdom from my experience to help others.

This magazine heals people from the articles alone and the energy of the people who produce this magazine, are angels.

Love to you all, and thank you for reading!

Patti Negri: Whenever possible I like to be prepared mentally, physically and psychically for my clients. (Well fed, rested, clear headed, focused, healthy, etc). It helps me be the best vessel for the information coming through.

Though if needed, I seem to be able to jump right in as needed.

I do like to always set my intent, create sacred space and be clear who or what energy or elements I invite in to help me during sessions!

Robert Rodriguez: I at times prepare for a psychic reading if instructed/asked to do so. However, the majority of the time psychic readings occur for me on a spontaneous basis i.e. at times it's as simple as someone just touching me and or visa versa, in sound so I'll get an instant message another example would be even if they happen to be speaking of a loved one whom has passed, the person has come through during the conversation.

Shannon Leischner: When giving a reading or conducting a healing session, there is an exchange of energy; during a session, I tap into a person's energy and they receive energy from me.
In order for me to keep myself from getting physically ill after a reading I must protect my energy.
I create a shield of white light and protection around me.
With practice, the creation of the shield is automatic when starting a reading, so I can be ready for a reading at a moments notice.
After the reading, I immediately cut the energy connection and send all of the residual energy to the light. Very often I will have clients come up to me and ask me if I remember saying such and such. I honestly let them know that I don't remember because I don't hold on to the energy of the readings. But when I tap into the energy of the person again I am instantly reminded of what I said and what happened in a previous reading. Protection and readings are like working a muscle, the more you do it, the better you become.

Jethro Smith: There are times when the guides spontaneously request that you read for someone.
However, as a principle, one must absolutely prepare in advance, and there are times when one should postpone a scheduled reading for a client, for example, a back-to-back reading where mediumship is involved is a clear example of a time to take time before the next client in order to "clear the energy."

April Ashbrook: I start my day by calling all my energy back and giving others people's energy back. Then chakra clears the way, every morning to put me on the right path. Then I call in sacred space with a prayer of protection. I'm ready. I do a tune up after a reading by clearing chakras, and sending back the energy I received.
I ground out all that's happened. I am always ready to listen to what my guides tell me.
Sometimes I ask them a question in front of the person and I'm comfortable with this! It's a great way to be! I've studied and took

classes, still studying and taking classes! I love how my life has improved others around me! One person at a time!!

John Cappello: The best answer to this question is "yes" and "no." Do I need to prepare for readings?
No. I am always available for a reading, however; I often try to get some rest before I read. Meditation is always a good thing to do prior to a session but it is not necessary to do this because the energy is always there to be sensed. I just have to allow myself to pay attention and the data is there for me to communicate.

Van Doren Figueredo: Yes, I do prepare myself before a session at all times and find my sacred space to be able receive information with much clarity. I also have experienced situations where a client has needed an emergency reading. I prepare myself with a deep 5 minute meditation to regroup and breathing to clear my energy.
As a professional psychic you will always need to be fully alert and keen with a balanced mental attitude to allow time for the next upcoming reading.

Chanda Reaves: I like always to start my day by practicing relaxation techniques, reciting mantras, and mediating prior to reading for my clients.
However, I do that for my own self protection against any astral nasties that may be attached to the questioner(s).
Auric and chakra cleansing are psychic calisthenics for any knowledgeable psychic or spiritually intuitive reader.
Psychic self-defense is of utmost importance when doing any type of psychic exercise or workings.
These continual practices allow me to read for my clients spontaneously without harm to myself.

Dena Flanagan: For me, it is a spontaneous process especially when I read on Psychics Gone Wild blog talk radio. On the radio show you have to be quick and you definitely do not have time to prepare for what is coming at you on the radio. I do not like to know anything about you before I do your reading, if I tune into your energy I will start getting things and I do not want to do that before the reading because my guides talk fast and full of information and I want you to hear and receive it all. I can read anybody at anytime once you ask.

do not want to read people without their permission so once you have initiated the process and you are ready then lots of information will come to you from my guides.

To begin my readings, I center in. To center in I take some deep breaths and then I call in my guides and surround myself with white light and loving protective energy, I then ask my guides to clear out all of my stuff and to bring you information for the best and highest good of all.

Melissa Berman: I always prepare for every session including radio and the like. The work is sacred and for me is to be respected in that way. It also provides protection from "uninvited" energy!

I prepare a special meditation for each client before our actual session ~ this is done with the client's permission as I am connecting to her/his spiritual team.

Sometimes, however, if I am speaking with someone, even on the street, and some guidance is asking to come through, I ask the person if I might share some information with her/him.

Most times, the person is receptive, and I, therefore, bring in the guidance as a gift to that person. However, if someone is not ready to receive whatever is coming through, then the wishes of that person are respected without question. Integrity is the key to all of this work.

*** *** ***

Part II
Listing of Trusted Lightworkers' Services and Areas of Practice

Listing Of Trusted Lightworkers' Services And Areas Of Practice

By Discipline/Specialty

A

Akashic records/Past life.
- Pamela Beaty, Reverend.

Angels Messenger.
- Corbie Mitleid, Reverend.
- Gliselda Amarillas-Ramirez.
- Jennifer Shackford.
- Patti Negri.
- Pennyc.
- Shannon Leischner.
- Suzanne Grace.

Animal Communicator.
- Bella Mason.
- Chris Avery Cole.
- Jennifer Wallens.
- Linda Salvin, Ph.D.
- Melissa A. Berman.
- Noelle Garneau.
- Patti Negri.

Aroma Therapy.
- Gliselda Amarillas-Ramirez.
- Patti Negri.

Astrology.
- April Ashbrook.
- Jethro Smith.
- Patrice Cole.

Aura Reading.
- Angeline Kim-Kyna Tan.
- Dina Vitantonio.
- Melissa Stamps.
- Robert Rodriguez, Reverend.

Auric Cleansing.
- Angeline Kim-Kyna Tan.
- Chanda Reaves, Reverend.
- Dina Vitantonio.
- Melissa Stamps.
- Patti Negri.

Caribbean Magick.
- Robert Rodriguez, Reverend.

Chakra Balancing.
- Angeline Kim-Kyna Tan.
- April Ashbrook.
- Chanda Reaves, Reverend.
- Chinhee Park.
- Dina Vitantonio.
- Jethro Smith.
- Melissa A. Berman.
- Melissa Stamps.
- Patti Negri.

Clairaudient.
- Chinhee Park.

- Chris Avery Cole.
- Le Vans Figueredo.
- Patti Negri.
- Robert Rodriguez, Reverend.
- Sunhee Park.

Clairsentient.
- Chinhee Park.
- Chris Avery Cole.
- Le Vans Figueredo.
- Patti Negri.
- Robert Rodriguez, Reverend.
- Sunhee Park.

Consultant.
- Chinhee Park.
- Georgia Marantos, MD.
- Linda Salvin, Ph.D
- Patti Negri.
- Robert Rodriguez, Reverend.
- Sunhee Park.

Crystal Ball Reading.
- Chanda Reaves, Reverend.
- Jethro Smith.
- Patti Negri.

Crystal Healing.
- Angeline Kim-Kyna Tan.
- Chanda Reaves, Reverend.
- Chinhee Park.
- Dina Vitantonio.
- Jennifer Shackford.
- Jethro Smith.
- Lynne Caddick.

- Patti Negri.

Custom Oils.
- Patti Negri.

Detective Psychic.
- Chris Avery Cole.

Dowsing.
- Chanda Reaves, Reverend.

Dreams' Interpretation.
- Chanda Reaves, Reverend.
- Kimberly Ward, Reverend.
- Linda Salvin, Ph.D.
- Pennyc.
- Van Doren Figueredo.

Elemental and Earth Magick.
- Patti Negri.

Empath.
- Bella Mason.
- Chinhee Park.
- Chris Avery Cole.
- Pamela Beaty, Reverend.
- Patti Negri.
- Robert Rodriguez, Reverend.
- Sunhee Park.
- Suzanne Grace.

Empathic Intuitive.
- Chinhee Park.

- Pamela Beaty, Reverend.
- Patti Negri.
- Sunhee Park.

Energy Designer.
- Melissa Stamps.

Energy Healer.
- Angela Bixby, Reverend.
- Angeline Kim-Kyna Tan.
- Chinhee Park.
- Dina Vitantonio.
- Gliselda Amarillas-Ramirez.
- Jennifer Wallens.
- Jethro Smith.
- Kimberly Ward, Reverend.
- Linda Salvin, Ph.D.
- Lynne Caddick.
- Melissa A. Berman.
- Melissa Stamps.
- Patti Negri.
- Robert Rodriguez, Reverend.
- Shannon Leischner.
- Sunhee Park.

ET Channeling.
- Robert Rodriguez, Reverend.
- Sunhee Park.
- Van Doren Figueredo.

Fairy Oracle.
- Gliselda Amarillas-Ramirez.

Feng Shui Consultations.

- Chanda Reaves, Reverend.
- Melissa Stamps.

Flower essences practitioner.
- Karina Voroshilova.

Healer (General).
- Chinhee Park
- Dena Flanagan.
- Dina Vitantonio.
- Georgia Marantos, MD.
- Karina Voroshilova.
- Melissa Stamps.
- Patti Negri.
- Sunhee Park.
- Suzanne Grace.

Holistic Counseling.
- Georgia Marantos, MD.
- Lisa Hurtt, Ph.D.

Intuitive Consultant.
- Angela Bixby, Reverend.
- Chinhee Park.
- Georgia Marantos, MD.
- Patti Negri.
- Sunhee Park.

Intuitive Spiritual Coach.
- Melissa A. Berman.
- Patti Negri.
- Sunhee Park.

Life Coaching.
- Angela Bixby, Reverend.
- Chinhee Park.
- Corbie Mitleid, Reverend.
- Jethro Smith.
- Kimberly Ward, Reverend.
- Le Vans Figueredo.
- Linda Carney.
- Linda Salvin, Ph.D.
- Lisa Hurtt, Ph.D.
- Melissa Stamps.
- Pamela Beaty, Reverend.
- Patrice Cole.
- Patti Negri.
- Pennyc.
- Shannon Leischner.
- Sunanda Sharma.
- Sunhee Park.
- Van Doren Figueredo.

Magick, Traditional.
- Patti Negri.

Mantras.
- Robert Rodriguez, Reverend.

Medical Intuitive.
- Jennifer Wallens.
- Jethro Smith.

Meditational Instruction Services.
- Chanda Reaves, Reverend.
- Jethro Smith.
- Linda Salvin, Ph.D.
- Patti Negri.

Medium.

- Angela Bixby, Reverend.
- Angeline Kim-Kyna Tan.
- April Ashbrook.
- Bella Mason.
- Chris Avery Cole.
- Corbie Mitleid, Reverend.
- Dena Flanagan.
- Janét Bowerman.
- Jennifer Wallens.
- Jethro Smith.
- John Cappello.
- Karina Voroshilova.
- Kimberly Ward, Reverend.
- Kristen Leona.
- Linda Carney.
- Linda Salvin, Ph.D.
- Lynne Caddick.
- Melissa A. Berman.
- Melissa Stamps.
- Pamela Beaty, Reverend.
- Patti Negri.
- Pennyc.
- Robert Rodriguez, Reverend.
- Sherie Roufosse.
- Sunhee Park.
- Suzanne Grace.
- Van Doren Figueredo.

Metaphysical Counseling Services.

- Chanda Reaves, Reverend.
- Corbie Mitleid, Reverend.
- Linda Salvin, Ph.D.
- Lisa Hurtt, Ph.D.
- Shannon Leischner.
- Van Doren Figueredo.

Metaphysical Healer.
- Linda Salvin, Ph.D.

Metaphysical Lectures and Seminars.
- Chanda Reaves, Reverend.
- Corbie Mitleid, Reverend.
- Linda Salvin, Ph.D.
- Lisa Hurtt, Ph.D.

Motivational Speaker.
- Patti Negri.
- Shannon Leischner.

Numerologist.
- April Ashbrook.
- Chanda Reaves, Reverend.
- Jennifer Wallens.
- Patrice Cole.

Oracle Card Reader.
- Kimberly Ward, Reverend.
- Patti Negri.

Palm Reader.
- Jethro Smith.

Paranormal Investigator.
- Jennifer Wallens.

Parapsychologist.
- Linda Salvin, Ph.D.

Past Life Retrieval and Analysis.
- Corbie Mitleid, Reverend.
- Jethro Smith.
- Pamela Beaty, Reverend.
- Patti Negri.
- Van Doren Figueredo.

Pendulum Readings.
- Angeline Kim-Kyna Tan.
- Chanda Reaves, Reverend.
- Patti Negri.
- Van Doren Figueredo.

Pet Psychic.
- Chris Avery Cole.
- Jennifer Wallens.

Photo Intuitive.
- Chris Avery Cole.

Psychic Artist.
- Jennifer Wallens.

Psychic Development.
- Chanda Reaves, Reverend.
- Jennifer Wallens.
- Kim-Kyna Tan.
- Linda Salvin, Ph.D.
- Lynne Caddick.
- Melissa A. Berman.
- Patti Negri.
- Shannon Leischner.
- Sunanda Sharma.
- Sunhee Park.

- Van Doren Figueredo.

Psychic Healing.
- Chinhee Park.
- Jethro Smith.
- Lynne Caddick.
- Patti Negri.
- Sunhee Park.

Psychic.
- Angela Bixby, Reverend.
- Angeline Kim-Kyna Tan.
- April Ashbrook.
- Bella Mason.
- Chanda Reaves, Reverend.
- Chinhee Park.
- Chris Avery Cole.
- Corbie Mitleid, Reverend.
- Dena Flanagan.
- Georgia Marantos, MD.
- Janét Bowerman.
- Jennifer Shackford.
- Jennifer Wallens.
- Jethro Smith.
- John Cappello.
- Karina Voroshilova.
- Kimberly Ward, Reverend.
- Kristen Lavespere.
- Kristen Leona.
- Linda Carney.
- Linda Salvin, Ph.D.
- Lisa Hurtt, Ph.D.
- Lynne Caddick.
- Melissa A. Berman.
- Melissa Stamps.
- Noelle Garneau.
- Patrice Cole.

- Patti Negri.
- Pennyc.
- Robert Rodriguez, Reverend.
- Shannon Leischner.
- Sherie Roufosse.
- Sunanda Sharma.
- Sunhee Park.
- Suzanne Grace.
- Van Doren Figueredo.

Psychometry.
- Melissa A. Berman.
- Melissa Stamps.
- Sunhee Park.

Reiki Healer.
- Gliselda Amarillas-Ramirez.
- Jennifer Shackford.
- Linda Salvin, Ph.D.
- Melissa A. Berman.
- Noelle Garneau.
- Sunanda Sharma.
- Suzanne Grace.

Reiki Master.
- Angela Bixby, Reverend.
- Angeline Kim-Kyna Tan.
- Chanda Reaves, Reverend.
- Kimberly Ward, Reverend.
- Suzanne Grace.

Remote Viewer.
- Chris Avery Cole.
- Linda Carney.
- Robert Rodriguez, Reverend.

- Sunhee Park.

Rituals.
- Patti Negri.

Shamanic bodywork.
- Melissa Stamps.

Shamanic Healing.
- Chanda Reaves, Reverend.
- Kimberly Ward, Reverend.
- Melissa Stamps.

Shamanic Practice.
- Kimberly Ward, Reverend.
- Robert Rodriguez, Reverend.

Shiatsu.
- Melissa Stamps.

Spiritual Advisor.
- Janét Bowerman.
- Pamela Beaty, Reverend.
- Patrice Cole.
- Patti Negri.
- Shannon Leischner.
- Sunanda Sharma.

Spells.
- Patti Negri.

Spiritual Guide.

- Corbie Mitleid, Reverend.
- Georgia Marantos, MD.
- Gliselda Amarillas-Ramirez.
- Jennifer Shackford.
- Noelle Garneau.
- Pamela Beaty, Reverend.
- Patti Negri.
- Pennyc.
- Shannon Leischner.

Spiritual Healing.
- Angeline Kim-Kyna Tan.
- Chinhee Park.
- Jennifer Wallens.
- Jethro Smith.
- Linda Salvin, Ph.D.
- Patti Negri.
- Robert Rodriguez, Reverend.
- Sunhee Park.

Spiritualist.
Linda Salvin, Ph.D.

Tarot Reading.
- April Ashbrook.
- Jethro Smith.
- Karina Voroshilova.
- Le Vans Figueredo.
- Lynne Caddick.
- Patti Negri.
- Robert Rodriguez, Reverend.
- Shannon Leischner.
- Sunanda Sharma.
- Van Doren Figueredo.

Tea Leaf Reader.

- Robert Rodriguez, Reverend.

Teacher.
- Dena Flanagan.
- Lynne Caddick.
- Patti Negri.
- Shannon Leischner.

Theta healer/instructor.
- Shannon Leischner.
- Suzanne Grace.

Trance Healing.
- Lynne Caddick.
- Melissa Stamps.
- Patti Negri.

Visionary.
- John Cappello.

*** *** ***

Listing Of Trusted Lightworkers' Services And Areas Of Practice

By Name

Angela Bixby, Reverend
- Energy Healer
- Intuitive Consultant
- Life Coach
- Medium
- Ordained Minister
- Psychic
- Reiki Master

Angeline Kim-Kyna Tan
- Auric Cleansing
- Chakra Balancing
- Crystal Healing
- Crystal Healing
- Medium
- Pendulum Readings
- Psychic
- Psychic Development
- Reiki Healing
- Spiritual Healing

April Ashbrook
- Astrology
- Medium
- Psychic
- Simple numerology
- Tarot
- Working with chakras

Bella Mason

- Animal Communicator
- Empath
- Medium
- Psychic

Chanda Reaves, Reverend

- Auric Cleansing
- Chakra Balancing
- Crystal Ball Reading
- Crystal Healing
- Dowsing
- Dreams' Interpretation
- Feng Shui Consultations
- Meditational Instruction Services
- Medium
- Metaphysical Counseling Services
- Metaphysical Lectures and Seminars
- Numerology
- Pendulum Readings
- Psychic
- Psychic Development
- Reiki Healing
- Shamanic Healing

Chinhee Park

- Crystal Healing
- Empath
- Energy Healing
- Life Coaching
- Medium
- Psychic
- Psychic Healing
- Spiritual Healing

Corbie Mitleid, Reverend

- Angels Messenger
- Spiritual Guide
- Life Coaching
- Medium
- Metaphysical Counseling Services
- Metaphysical Lectures and Seminars
- Past Life Retrieval and Analysis
- Psychic

Chris Avery Cole
- Clairaudient
- Clairsentient
- Clairvoyant
- Detective Psychic
- Empath
- Medium
- Pet
- Photo Intuitive
- Psychic
- Remote Viewer

Dena Flanagan
- Healer
- Medium
- Psychic
- Teacher

Dina Vitantonio
- Auric Cleansing
- Chakra Balancing
- Crystal Healing
- Energy's Healing

Georgia Marantos, MD
- Consultant
- Healer

- Intuitive
- Ordained Spiritualist Minister
- Psychic
- Spirit-guided readings
- Teacher

Gliselda Amarillas-Ramirez
- Angels Messenger
- Aroma Therapy
- Energy's Healing
- Fairy Oracle
- Pendulum Readings
- Psychic
- Reiki Healing
- Spiritual Guide

Janét Bowerman
- Life Coach
- Psychic
- Reiki healer
- Spiritual advisor

Jennifer Shackford
- Angels Messenger
- Crystal Healing
- Psychic
- Reiki Healing
- Spiritual Guide

Jennifer Wallens
- Animal Communicator
- Energy Practitioner,
- Medical Intuitive
- Medical Intuitive
- Medium

- Numerologist
- Paranormal Investigator
- Pet Psychic
- Psychic
- Psychic Artist
- Psychic Development
- Spiritual Healing

Jethro Smith
- Astrology
- Chakra Balancing
- Crystal Ball Reading
- Crystal Healing
- Energy's Healing
- Life Coaching
- Medical Intuitive
- Meditational Instruction Services
- Medium
- Palm Reader
- Past Life Retrieval and Analysis
- Psychic
- Psychic Healing
- Spiritual Healing
- Tarot Reader

John Cappello
- Medium
- Psychic
- Visionary

Karina Voroshilova
- Flower essences practitioner
- Healer
- Medium
- Psychic
- Tarot Reader

Kimberly Ward, Reverend
- Dream Interpreter
- Energy Therapist
- Life Coaching
- Medium
- Oracle Card Reader,
- Psychic
- Reiki Master, Level III Integrated
- Shamanic Practitioner

Kristen Lavespere
- Psychic

Kristen Leona
- Medium
- Psychic

Le Vans Figueredo
- Clairaudient
- Clairsentient
- Clairvoyant
- Life Coach
- Psychic
- Tarot Card Reader

Linda Carney
- Intuitive Life Coach
- Medium
- Psychic
- Remote Viewer

Linda Salvin, Ph.D
- Animal Communicator
- Dreams' Interpretation

- Energy's Healing
- Life Coaching
- Meditational Instruction Services
- Medium
- Metaphysical Counseling Services
- Metaphysical healer
- Metaphysical Lectures and Seminars
- Parapsychologist
- Psychic
- Psychic Development
- Reiki Healing
- Spiritual Healing
- Spiritualist

Lisa Hurtt, Ph.D
- Holistic Counseling
- Life Coaching
- Metaphysical Counseling Services
- Metaphysical Lectures and Seminars
- Psychic

Lynne Caddick
- Crystal Healing
- Energy's Healing
- Medium
- Psychic
- Psychic Development
- Psychic Healing

Melissa A. Berman
- Animal Communicator
- Chakra Balancing
- Energy's Healing
- Intuitive Spiritual Coach
- Medium
- Psychic

- Psychic Development
- Psychometry
- Reiki Healing

Melissa Stamps
- Auric Cleansing
- Chakra Balancing
- Clairvoyance
- Energy Designer
- Energy's Healing
- Feng Shui Consultations
- Hypnotherapy
- Life Coaching
- Medium
- Past life regression
- Professional Interior Designer
- Psychic
- Psychometry
- Shamanic bodywork
- Shamanic Healing
- Shiatsu
- Trance healing

Noelle Garneau
- Angels Messenger/Spiritual Guide
- Psychic
- Reiki Healing

Pamela Beaty, Reverend
- Empathic Intuitive
- Licensed Minister
- Medium
- Past life/Akashic records
- Spirit Channeler
- Spiritual Life Coach

Patrice Cole
Astrology
Life Coaching
Numerology
Psychic
Spiritual Advisor

Patti Negri
Angels Messenger
Animal Communicator
Auric Cleansing
Chakra Balancing
Clairvoyant
Crystal Ball Reading
Crystal Healing
Custom Oils
Elemental and Earth Magick
Empath
Energy's Healing
House Blessing
House Clearing
Lecturing
Life Coaching
Magick
Meditational Instruction Services
Medium
Metaphysical Counseling Services
Pendulum Readings
Psychic
Psychic Development
Psychic Healing
Rituals
Spells
Spiritual Guide
Tarot Card Reader
Teaching

Pennyc
- Angels Messenger/Spiritual Guide
- Dreams' Interpretation

- Life Coaching
- Medium
- Psychic

Robert Rodriguez, Reverend
- Aura Reading
- Caribbean Magick
- Clairaudient
- Clairsentient
- Clairvoyant
- Empathic
- Energy Healing
- ET Channeling
- Mantras
- Medium
- Psychic
- Remote Viewing
- Shaman
- Spiritual Healing
- Tarot Card Reader
- Tea Leaf Reader

Sunhee Park
- Clairaudient
- Crystal Healing
- Energy Healer
- ESP
- ET Channeler
- Life Coaching
- Medium
- Psychic
- Psychic Healing
- Psychometry
- Spiritual Healing

Shannon Leischner
- Angel communicator

- Energy Healer
- Life Path Coach
- Medium
- Motivational Speaker
- Psychic
- Spiritual counselor
- Tarot Reader
- Theta healer/instructor

Sherie Roufosse.
- Psychic
- Medium

Sunanda Sharma
- Author
- Life coach
- Psychic
- Reiki Healer
- Spiritual Counselor
- Tarot reader

Suzanne Grace
- Angel Practitioner
- Empath
- Medium
- Psychic
- Reconnective Healer
- Reiki
- Theta Healer

Van Doren Figueredo
- Dreams' Interpretation
- ET Channeler
- Life Coaching
- Medium

- Metaphysical Counseling Services
- Past Life Retrieval and Analysis
- Pendulum Readings
- Psychic
- Psychic Development
- Tarot Card Reader

*** *** ***

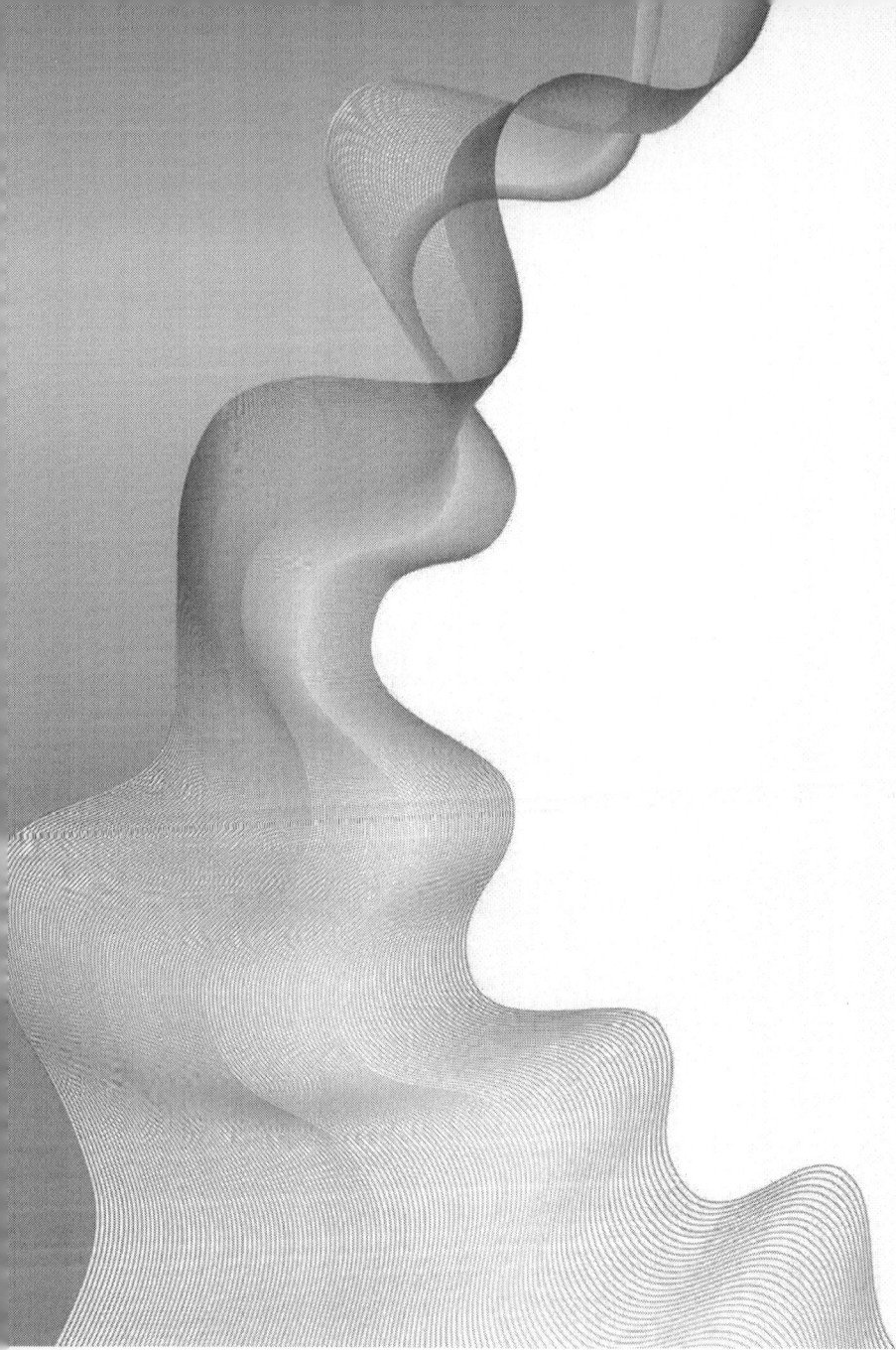

PART III
Profile of the Most Trusted Lightworkers

Publishers' Note:

Although verified, lightworkers' statements, claims and profiles are herewith reproduced "As Is", meaning, published verbatim, as received, and intentionally unedited, in order to preserve their originality and authenticity.

*** *** ***

Intuition is simply an expanded listening, something we all have access to.
-Reverend Angela Bixby

Reverend Angela Bixby
Certified by the American Federation of Certified Psychics and
Mediums. New York.

Contact: energyintuit@gmail.com;
Phone: 302-345-0575

Websites: www.energyintuit.com; www.facebook.com/energyintuit

Specialty: Psychic, Medium, Energy Healer, Reiki Master, Intuitive Consultant, Ordained Minister, Life Coach.

Years of practice/experience: 20 informally, 5 formally.

Languages: English.

Profile: Living beyond the five senses has always been a part of how Angela Bixby sees and approaches the world.
She is a Certified Psychic Medium with the American Federation of Certified Psychics and Mediums, which has deepened her natural intuitive abilities that she gained at a young age. Angela is a Certified Reiki Master and Energy Healer for her clients as well. Angela offers healing and guidance to your questions by bridging angelic & spirit realms, dreamtime, energetic fields and our own physical world.
Her passion is helping people to trust their own intuition by offering insight into past, present and future events.
Angela Bixby holds a BA in Psychology from the University of Minnesota and formerly worked in healthcare.
Angela is working on a memoir and is the mother of two spirited, young men in Wilmington, Delaware.

Featured in: American Psychic & Medium, August 2013 issue.

Rates/Fees:
- $120/hour
- $75/30 minutes

Personal message or philosophy: "Intuition is simply an expanded listening, something we all have access to."

**Working with compassion and love,
rather than sympathy, is one
of my universal laws.**
-April Ashbrook

April Ashbrook
Certified by the American Federation of Certified Psychics and
Mediums. New York.

Contact: aprilashbrook@icloud.com
Phone number: 925-848-7079.

Preferred time to contact: 11-7 PST.

Specialty: Psychic, medium, working with chakras, astrology, tarot and simple numerology.

Years of practice/experience: Worked with tarot for 10+ years, worked professionally since 2009

Languages: English.

Profile: I am a certified psychic and medium through Higher Source International and the American Federation of certified Psychics & Mediums. As a happily married wife with three wonderful children! I have been given the gift and privilege to contribute to the world in a special way. After three near death experiences, I found myself experiencing higher vibrations than ever before, opening my third eye to a whole new world.

My strongest ability is to open and clear blockages in chakras throughout the body with the help of Spirit.
I channel the Archangels and Ascended masters for extra help in clearing and healing blockages. I have been working with tarot cards for over ten years, and I am working toward proficiency in both numerology and astrology.
As a medium, I am able to channel archangels and ascended masters, as well as my spirit guides, in order to provide a more accurate reading into one's life to decipher what healing is needed at any given time.
Everyone is born with the gift of clairvoyance, but the pressures of everyday life and the outside world often influence these people to forget. I help them remember how to get back in touch with their own souls and spirit guides, promoting a happier and healthier life path.

My natural healing ability helps others remove the blockages of fear and guilt that they carry from the past, or even past lives, so they are more open to loving themselves. My true purpose in this life is to help people learn to love themselves, so they may learn to love others just as much.

Featured in: American Psychic Medium Magazine, February 2014 issue.

Rates/Fees:
- $50 for 30 minutes.
- $80 for 1 hour.

Payment expected prior to service; refund can be given after first 5 minutes. Accept cash, check, and PayPal payments.

Personal message: You must love yourself before you can love others. My mission is to heal wounds as a victim and help people build on weaknesses to turn them into strengths so they can look in the mirror and truthfully say they love themselves.

Working with compassion and love, rather than sympathy, is one of my universal laws. I built boundaries with my spirit guide to help me stay on a clear path with the knowledge I need to share with my clients.

*** *** ***

Stop being the victim of destiny
and connect with the
Universal Divine.
-Reverend Chanda Lea Reaves

Rev. Chanda Lea Reaves, B. Msc., AAS, CMA (AAMA)
Certified by the American Federation of Certified Psychics and
Mediums. New York.

Contact: Phone: (402) 957-1873 Office
E-Mail: chanda@chan-wan.com
Websites: http://www.chanwan.com ; http://starseedfederatio
n.webs.com

Areas of Practice: Empathic Spiritual Intuitive, Psychic,
Medium, Clairvoyant, Remote Viewer, Tarot Master, Dream
Weaving, Dream Interpretation, L-Rod /Pendulum Dowsing and
Scrying, Metaphysical Practitioner, Metaphysical Counseling
Services, Metaphysical Lectures and Seminars, Meditational
Instruction Services, Feng Shui Consultations, Cosmic Telepathy
Usui Reiki Grandmaster, Usui Shiki Reiki Ryoho Master, AMA
Deus Shamanic Healer, Crystal Healer, Numerology, Esoteric
Astrology, Channelings, Automatic Writings.

Awards:
- Usui Shiki Reiki Ryoho Master. Levels 1,2,3 - Practice,
  Instruction, Attunements

- National Board Certified and Tested: Psychic, Medium, Metaphysician, Healer, Remote Viewer and Tarot Master.
- AMA Deus Shamanic Healing Master.
- The International Library of Poetry: Distinguished Poet, Published Poet - Metaphysical Poetry 2006.

Membership:
- American Federation of Certified Psychics and Mediums, Inc., March 7th, 2013.
- Holistic Healers Academy (HHA), May 16th, 2008. Usui Reiki Master.
- Australian Metaphysical Association (AMpA) - March 28th, 2008.
- World Reiki Association (WRA), March 10th, 2008.
- Order of the Eastern Star: Grand Lodge State of New York, Manhattan District, Alpha Chapter #1, April 2, 2005.
- Rosicrucian Fellowship - November 7, 2005.
- American Tarot Association, November 1, 2005, Member.

Languages: English.

Biography: Born a spiritually gifted child and being Creole (Native American, Jamaican, Haitian, Irish and French), Reverend Chanda hails from a long family line of spiritualists from Mississippi, Louisiana, Jamaica and Haiti.
As a 4th generation psychic, Chanda Reaves' teachings esteem from her paternal grandmother who was an experienced and accurate spiritualist and psychic mentoring her in developing her psychic ability from the age of twelve.
Chanda Reaves' spiritual background consists of Metaphysics: Christ, Buddha and Krishna Consciousness, Guaraní Native American Shamanism and Creole teachings.
As an Ordained Metaphysical Minister through International Metaphysical Ministries, she has been living, understanding and developing spiritual gifts for over 25 years.
Throughout Chanda's life path, she has had a multitude of paranormal experiences, extraterrestrial abduction/contacts, and Ascended Master visitations.

On July 17th, 1994, at approximately 9:30 pm CST USA, she had an encounter of the fourth kind with 17 hours of missing time and returned to her place of abduction and contact approximately 1:30 pm, the subsequent afternoon; retaining full memory of the abduction/contact experience and physical markings.

Over a two year span, from March 2005-2007, she was repeatedly contacted and downloaded, in New Rochelle, New York.

June 6th, 2007, Rev. Chanda was again contacted, scanned and downloaded with universal knowledge of the highest order by the Biaviian Council.

October 31st, 2008, United Starseed Federation was telepathically channeled by Rev. Chanda from Rayshondra of the Nibiruan Council.

July 23rd, 2009, in Omaha Nebraska, with multiple witnesses present, an encounter of the third kind took place with a massive download that occurred over a seven minute period. November 4th, 2009, in Omaha, Nebraska, she was visited and downloaded by the Sirian Council.

On multiple occasions, there have been witnesses present and experiencers during these encounters.

These prolific life changing abductions and contact events, not only enhanced her intuitive abilities; it has also expanded universal awareness and life's mission to assist many other Hybrids, Starseeds, Lightworkers, Grid workers, Crystal and Indigo Children to adjust and prepare for their own life's missions and ascension processes. Over the years, Rev. Chanda has been contacted both telepathically and physically with evident scoop marks, implants, massive downloads, channelings and automatic writings.

She has dedicated her life's mission to counseling and support of others sharing in these similar experiences.

Featured in:
- American Psychic & Medium Magazine: Issues August 2013, February 2014.
- United States National Register of Tested, Certified and Bona Fide Lightworkers, Psychics and Mediums: 2013 Editions.
- Parapsychology & Mind Power Magazine, Issue 2 2013.
- International Library of Poetry's Anthology 'Timeless Voices'. Published poem: 'Evergreen Seldom Seen', 2006.
- Ehow.com Contributor: 'How to Prepare for a Reiki Attunement.'
- Demand Studios, Inc.: Author, Writer.

- The Witches Keen Group by Christian Day.

Radio Appearances:
Dr. Linda Salvin, Ph.D. Radio Show.
Karen Kinsey's Meta-Stories Radio Show.

Rates/Fees:
- Metaphysical Counseling: $75.00/hour
- Reiki Attunements: $25.00/Attunement
- Crystal Healing: $35.00/ 30 minute session
- Usui Reiki i, II, & III Course of Instruction: $77.77
- AMA Deus Course of Instruction: $77.77
- 15 minute readings - $20.00 Web Special
- 30 minute readings - $40.00
- 60 minute readings - $75.00

Personal Philosophy: "Stop being the victim of destiny and connect with the Universal Divine Conscious Collective from within to fully experience the richness of your soul's magnificent journey. Be the Co-Creator of your own existence and experience it to the fullest."

*** *** ***

I intend to evolve to the highest level
and live at the highest vibrations.
That is what's going to help
heal this world.
It all begins with you.
- Chinhee Park

Chinhee Park

Certified by the American Federation of Certified Psychics and Mediums. New York.

Contact: Chinhee@ESPsychics.com
Phone: 347.826.1425
Website: www.ESPsychics.com

Specialties: Psychic, Medium, Empath, Energy Healer.

Years of practice/experience: 15

Languages: English, Italian and Spanish

Profile:
Both Chinhee and her twin-sister Sunhee recognized their gifts of clairvoyance, empathy, telepathy, and mediumship at a young age. At 15, they both had the same dream of their mother dying from Cancer. Their prediction came true shortly after. At 19, the twins started to exercise more of their abilities within the entertainment industry. It was during this time that they were spotted in the streets of Manhattan by an NBA basketball player and talent agent.

This talent agent sent them on auditions for small parts in Law & Order, MTV, TBS, Independent Films as psychics, Estee Lauder Shoot, Got Milk Twins, Marie Claire Magazine, Book of Twins, Time, People, and many other international magazines and newspapers. That was an amazing experience for these two small town girls.

This lead to finding themselves taking an interest in what was taking place behind the scenes and as a result soon took over their agent's business. This agent was amazed at their ability to know what actors or models were going to get booked for a specific project.

At 21, they were considered the youngest talent managers in the industry and the only company who specialized with "ethnic" and "real" people.

The twins also worked for a boutique business management firm that represented A-list celebrities such as Raquel Welch, Judy Collins, NBA Basketball Stars, actors/models/artists.

They also did aerial photography by hanging out of a Robinson R22 helicopter without a door.

They shot riots, celebrity weddings, news coverage, the O.J. case and so on. Sunhee worked with NY-1 News assisting the Celebrity reporter for high society events, and movie premieres while Chinhee was at Paramount Pictures helping Don Johnson in casting his TV series.

Their path took them to where they are today in the spiritual world.

Chinhee and Sunhee Park are in the process of creating their own television show a TV series displaying their psychic gifts and personal lives of tragedy turned into triumph.

http://youtu.be/IfdLLf_kl28

Awards received:

- 2013: Voted #3 Best Psychic in the U.S. and #3 in the world.
- Graced the cover of "Parapsychology & Mind Power" magazine.
- Graced the cover of "American Psychic" magazine.
- 2012: Voted # 1 Best Psychic in the U.S. with Patti Negri. Voted #3 Best Psychic in the World. Cover of Book: "International Register for the World's Best Psychics, Mediums, Astrologer, Light Workers. Volume II. In addition, she graced the cover of the French version of this book.
- 2012: Voted #3 by for the International Register of the United States for Best Psychics Book.
- 2012: Voted as one of "The Most Caring Psychics in the World".
- 2012: Voted as one of the top 5 Best Psychics and Mediums in the world, by UFOs and Supernatural magazine, issue.
- 2011: Certified Psychic by The American Federation of Certified Psychics and Mediums.
- 2011: Sunhee made top 12 Psychic in the world in "The Battle of The Psychics" television show in the Ukraine.

She declined the contract to do her own television show in the states with her sister.

Featured in:

- The United States and the World's Best Psychics, Mediums, Healers, Astrologers, Palmists, Witches and Tarot Readers 2013-2014.
- 2012: Appointed Chief Examiners of "The American Federation of Certified Psychics and Mediums".
- 2012: Graced the cover of "Art, UFO & Supernatural" Magazine with fellow psychic Patti Negri.
- 2012: Graced the cover of Bellesprit magazine.
- 2012: Chinhee and her sister Sunhee are featured in a new book about "Bullying" by Jill Vanderwood. They will be featured in her "celebrity section" of bullying stories.

In 2010, the twins hosted their own radio show on CBS for over 2 years. Apart from hosting a show, they have also been guests on Mothership Radio, LA Talk, various CBS radio shows, and several others. In 2010, the twins were invited to offer their gifts for the 2011 Feb. Grammy Award presenters and nominees.
Their certificates will be placed in the SWAG bags for Celine Dion, Kelly Preston, and Mariah Carey's baskets. All thanks to HollywoodBaskets.com owned by Lisa Gal Bianchi.

Rates/Fees: $225.00/Hr. Discount for first time clients

Personal message: "My mission is to help people. I've always known this was my purpose in life ever since I was young. I've always felt good knowing I had a purpose in life.
This purpose helped me to endure the dark times and struggles. I have come a long way, and now I'm here to help others.
I work on myself everyday, taking care of my mind, body and soul. I intend to evolve to the highest level and live at the highest vibrations. That is what's going to help heal this world.
It all begins with you."

*** *** ***

Nobody should have to go through
this life in pain or heartache
or confused and instead should
be living it with joy and
love and lightness.-
Dena Flanagan

Dena Flanagan
Certified by the American Federation of Certified Psychics and Mediums. New York.

Contact: Email: essenceot@aol.com
Phone: 207-752-1399
Website: denaflanaganpsychicmedium.com

Specialty: Psychic/Medium/Healer/Teacher.

Years of practice/experience: 28 years.

Languages: English.

Profile: Dena lives on the coast of Maine and has been helping people with her many gifts for the past 28 years.
Dena was born with the gifts of hearing (clairaudient), seeing images (clairvoyant), feeling the truth (clairsentient) and is able to talk to your passed on loved ones (medium). In addition she has the gifts of healing and works on a deep soul level and is a truly gifted teacher.
As a psychic, she calls in her spirit guides and they communicate with your spirit guides to bring you the information you need to

get clear concise answers to help you on your path of greatness.
Her guides are very talkative and they love to give you lots of information on any question you might have.

She specializes in people and has the ability to see inside of other people's minds, heart and soul as well as yours, which enables her to help you with relationships whether it is love, family, workmates/boss, friends, children or associates.

Other areas of specialty are work-career, finances, health, finding your soul purpose, identifying your past lives and how they relate to this life. The information that comes through is usually amazing, transformative and quite accurate.

As a medium, Dena can talk to people who have passed on. She will call in the person you wish to talk to and in the process they usually use her body as a tool to come through and speak (like channeling them through). She gives you the messages that they are wanting to get through to you, and the messages are personal to you and what they want or need you to hear. This process usually brings you the peace and comfort that you need to move through your grief or to bring you answers to questions you might have.

As a healer, she is a Reiki Master and has used that as a basis for her healings to do her deep soul work, she has the ability to see what you need to live your life to your full potential without all the blockages and fears holding you back. When she does her healing work, she calls in her guides, angels, the archangels and passed on loved ones to assist.

They in turn use her body as an instrument to go in and remove the blockages and fears as well as all the negative emotions you carry with you on a subconscious soul level.

These sessions will bring you peace, lightness, joy and the ability to live with light and love and get you back onto your true path.

She can do them long distance or in person and has helped many with health problems, cancer, heart problems, anxiety, depression and many other things.

As a teacher, Dena has taught many classes over the years and works with people one on one as well as groups to bring them to a place of using their intuition & psychic abilities and to learn to listen to their spirit guides. She has taught a variety of subjects such as "Psychic Development" and "Learning How to Read the Tarot". Her uncanny ability to find the way you learn the best and her way of communicating is amazing.

She uses a variety of ways to teach because we all learn different or we all have different strengths that need to be recognized and brought out, some people hear the message, some people see the visions, and some people feel or sense it and you will know which one is your strength when you take a class or lesson with Dena.

Over the course of the 28 years Dena has studied many subjects such as tarot, psychic development, reiki, various ways of healing, palmistry, numerology, astrology, psychometry, tea leaf reading, past life regression, shamanic journeying, tapping, working with your chakras, auras, angel energy, spirit guides, automatic writing, crystals and crystal healing, soul healing, pendulum, animal totems, releasing energy blocks, protections exercises, muscle testing, visualization and manifestation, power of positive thinking, meditation, affirmations, interpretation of dreams, acupressure, labyrinth, scrying (crystal ball reading), casting stones, bringing your intuitive thoughts to canvas, drawing your spirit guides, vision boards, mandalas, eye iridology, channeling, chanting, and animal communication

Dena has helped many and has read everybody from the rich and famous to people who need it for free all over the world. She has run many psychic fairs, read on cruise ships, corporate parties, read on the radio and is currently reading on blog talk radio for "Psychics gone wild" as well as for her many private clients she has.

Awards received:
- Certified Reiki Master.
- Certified Psychic.
- Certified Medium.

Featured in: Dena Flanagan has been featured in many newspaper articles and magazines over the years and the ones as of late are the August 2013 and February 2014 "American Psychic and Medium Magazine", and "Art, UFOs & Supernatural Magazine" 2013.

Rates/Fees:
- $55.00 per 1/2 hour.
- $100.00 per hour.

Dena offers readings in person, over the phone, Skype or email as well as house parties, privately and in groups and galleries for both the psychic and medium work. She offers healings in person or distant healing.

Personal message: Dena was given this beautiful gift to help people in this life to become lighter and to make it her mission to do so. She has seen so many miracles and blessings come from using her gift and sharing it with the world.

Her belief is that nobody should have to go through this life in pain or heartache or confused and instead should be living it with joy and love and lightness. When you are on your true path that was intended for you then you will feel these great feelings and with her guidance from her spirit guides she will help you to get to that awesome place.

She is very gifted and has a wonderful way with people and truly enjoys what she does. Whether you get a psychic reading, a medium reading, a healing or take lessons from her you will walk away with a feeling of love & lightness from her caring wisdom and gifts.

*** *** ***

Helping by sharing.
-Gliselda Amarillas

Gliselda Amarillas

Certified by the American Federation of Certified Psychics and Mediums. New York.

Contact: Email: gamarillas33@gmail.com
Phone: 619-392-6675

Specialty: Psychic, Empath, Clairvoyant, Clairsentience, Usui Reiki/Karuna Reiki Master, Distance Healing, Numerologist, Deeksha Oneness Blessing Giver, Fairy Oracle/Angel Tarot card reader, and Aromatherapy consultant

Years of practice/experience: 9 years.

Languages: English and Spanish

Featured in: Art, UFO, & Supernatural Magazine Vol.1 Issue 8.

Fees/Rates:
- Reiki session $65
- 30 minute Reading $45
- 30 minute Counseling $45
- 1 E-mail question $20

Autobio: She feels very grateful and blessed to be able to help people better understand their life and the different approaches there is and also how to understand and live with love, light, and peace of mind!
Gliselda Amarillas is the 5th child of 5 girls.
She was very perceptive since childhood, but didn't know that it was such a special God given gift, that she tried to ignore it. It was later in her late 20's when she had to battle with cancer, go through a couple of surgery, and 8 months of chemo, that made her gifts stronger, because she was afraid of not being there for her 3 year old son and maybe not seeing him grow up. The idea of having to face death really set her in the spiritual path. At first she became very sensitive and would follow her intuition even though it was overwhelming for her because she really didn't know exactly what it was.
She would know things and didn't know how but she just knew and people would ask: How do you know?

And she didn't know how to explain it. These gifts were not only becoming stronger but even clearer. She feels that this gives her an opportunity to help by sharing what she knows, and with this "Pay It Forward" by helping those in need of spiritual guidance.

Philosophy: Helping by sharing.

*** *** ***

Uphold the highest of authenticity
and integrity.
-Janét Bowerman

Janét Bowerman aka Braveheart Butterfly

Contact: braveheartbutterfly@gmail.com; Little Rock, AR
Website: www.braveheartbutterfly.com

Specialty: Psychic, Spiritual advisor, Life Coach, Reiki healer.

Years of practice/experience 20+

Language: English

Profile: Janét Bowerman, aka as 'Braveheart Butterfly' is a natural born intuitive empath/clairsentient. She also has the ability to hear (clairaudient) and see (clairvoyant). She is a gifted channeler and spirit messenger specializing in relationships, life coaching, Reiki healing, and self-growth.
She has the ability to read energy when looking at photographs. Janét communicates with spirit and works with her spirit guides to give accurate messages and advice to to life questions. She has a degree in Psychology and is a certified Reiki practitioner and a certified Doreen Virtue angel card reader. Janét is a professional psychic for ESPsychics, Bellesprit Magazine and Keen.
She offers readings by appointment for those seeking guidance.

Featured in: Bellesprit Magazine as a Diamond Psychic as well as a Professional Psychic on ESPsychic website.

Rates:
- 15 min - $35
- 30 min - $60
- 60 minutes - $110
- $20 - One question email
- $35 - Two question email
- Life Coaching sessions - $99/hr

Payments made in advance thru Paypal

My philosophy: By upholding the highest of authenticity and integrity, I use my gifts to assist and guide others on their life's journey along with providing Spiritual and Intuitive guidance.

Life and love are truly everlasting.
-Jennifer Wallens

Jennifer Wallens

Certified by the American Federation of Certified Psychics and Mediums. New York.

Contact: Jenniferwallens@icloud.com;
Phone: 702-334-6675

Website: www.JenniferWallens.com

Specialty: Psychic, Medium, Animal Communicator, Pet Psychic, Psychic Artist, Energy Practitioner, Numerologist, Paranormal Investigator, and Medical Intuitive

Years of practice/experience: 22

Languages: English

Biography: Jennifer Wallens, BA, (Rollins College) Certified Spiritualist Psychic Medium, Spirit/Psychic Artist, Animal Communicator, Energy Practitioner, Numerologist, Paranormal Investigator and Medical Intuitive. Jennifer Wallens has been a trusted and caring evidential Psychic Medium and teacher for over 22 years.

She also has over 25 years experience as a Environmental Scientist/Biologist and is very much concerned with obtaining evidence and facts regarding proof of life after death.

She was trained in the Spiritualist tradition and is grateful for this disciplined training which allowed her to learn from the very best ethical and evidential mediums in the world.

Jennifer is Certified through the AFCPM, and has been voted #1 Animal Communicator in the World, as well as #2 Medium and #3 Psychic in the World and USA in 2013-2014.

Jennifer is a member of the (SNU) Spiritualists National Union, the SNUI-International (SNUI) and also featured in the ESPsychics.com and Best Psychic Directory and listed in the top 5 of America's Best Psychics and Mediums. Jennifer, also known as Дженнифер Уолленс in the Ukraine & Russia, was selected as one of the top 4 Psychics in the Worldwide competition on the popular TV show "Battle of the Psychics -War of the Worlds", Битва экстрасенсов on the STB Channel in 2011.

She was also chosen as "Best Psychic" of week 5 by the jurors during the filming of the series.

Aside from her 6 months of filming the TV series in the Ukraine, Jennifer has traveled extensively demonstrating her mediumship abilities in front of live audiences and on several radio programs.

She will be touring the US, UK and Australia in 2014-2015. Jennifer Wallens has had psychic ability since childhood, sensing the spirit world, clairsentiently, clairaudiently, and clairvoyantly. An affinity with nature and communicating with animals led Jennifer to receive her BA degree in Environmental Studies at Rollins College in 1985.

In the following years she trained as a Medium at the Cassadaga Camp Meeting Association in Florida, as well as many intensive week long courses in Mediumship and Healing at the famed College of Psychic Studies, Arthur Findlay College in Stansted, Mountfitchett UK.

Jennifer has completed several other workshops both in the USA and UK and continues to train whenever possible. Most recently with Angelic Healing training through the "Seraphim Blueprint" method, as well as Past Life Regression.

Jennifer believes no one should ever stop learning and striving to improve their abilities to better serve. Jennifer is also a part of experimental Physical Trance and Mental Mediumship exercises with a group around the world and continues to work on her Trance and Healing mediumship as well. She is currently working on her first book and set of Development CDs.

Awards received if applicable:
  Jennifer was just voted #1 Best Animal Communicator in the World, and USA;
  She is also ranked #2 in the World & USA as Best Medium;
  And #3 in the World & USA as Best Psychic in the National and International Election/Vote of the USA and World's Best Mediums, Psychics, Healers, Pet Psychics/Animal Communicators, Palmists, by Times Square Press, New York for 2013-2014.

Jennifer, also known as Дженнифер Уолленс in the Ukraine & Russia, was selected as one of the top 4 Psychics in the Worldwide competition on the popular TV show "Battle of the Psychics -War of the Worlds", Битва экстрасенсов on the STB Channel in 2011

AMERICAN PSYCHIC & MEDIUM

JANUARY 2014 ISSUE

2013-2014 WORLD'S BEST PSYCHICS, MEDIUMS, HEALERS ASTROLOGERS, TAROT READERS, LIGHTWORKERS.

THE GREAT
FE WALLENS:
VOTED #1
COMMUNICATO
WOR

Patti Negri's American
Federation of Certified
Psychics and Mediums

Jennifer Wallens on the cover of American Psychic & Medium
Magazine, January 2014 Issue.

Featured in:

> Jennifer was featured on the January 2014 cover of American Psychic and Medium Magazine,
>
> The book "The United States and the World's Best Psychics, Mediums, Healers, Astrologers, Palmists, Witches and Tarot Readers 2013-2014.
>
> Jennifer was also honored by being put on the cover of a 2012 book "America's & world's best psychics & healers who care most about you".

Additional publications and videos featuring Jennifer can be found on her website on her Media Page.
http://www.jenniferwallens.com/media.html

Rates/Fees: Jennifer offers:

- 30 and 60 min Psychic Only readings, by Phone or Skype
- 60 min Psychic Mediumship readings, by phone or Skype which involve communication with those who have passed over into the Afterlife, as well as psychic information for any questions or concerns you may have.
- 90 min Spirit Portrait Auragraphs by phone or Skype which include a 60 minute Mediumship reading, as well as a finished Auragraph which is rendered in pastel and is mailed to you. 60 min.
- 60 min Animal Communication Sessions are by phone or Skype or in-person.
- Small Group events are in person and may have from 3-10 people
- Larger Group Events can be arranged, Please call her office (702-334-6675) to schedule these.

Jennifer's current rates and fees for each particular service 30 min. or 60 min. can be found on her website services page. Jennifer also donates her time for several readings each month for those in need that cannot pay, please email her if you wish to be considered for a free reading.
http://www.jenniferwallens.com/services.html.

Personal message:
"I have always felt humbled to be a Psychic Medium and Animal Communicator and to be asked to connect with my clients and their loved ones with and without fur. Imagine being a guest at a loving family reunion, this is how I feel during a reading. I am honored to be able to feel the love and hear the words that bring

such comfort, often, it is hard not to be overwhelmed. I can only strive to convey messages from those in spirit as accurately as possible, to show that life and love are truly everlasting, and to do so as long as God allows me to be of service.

I am so grateful for my gifts and I hope to be able to also help more people use their own gifts to enrich their lives, and heal those emotional wounds. Namaste."

*** *** ***

One should always test the spirits
to ensure they are staying in the light
in according with one's belief
in the Higher Power.
-Reverend Jethro Smith

Reverend Jethro Smith
Certified by the American Federation of Certified Psychics and
Mediums. New York.

Contact: psychicjethro@aol.com
Phone: 928-284-0437
Website: http://www.jethrosmith.net/

Specialty: Psychic, Palm Reader, Tarot Reader, Astrology.

Years of practice/experience: 30 years.

Languages: English.

Profile: Reverend Jethro Smith, part Native American Indian, is a natural-born intuitive whose gift heightened dramatically after a near-death experience.
In kindergarten, Jethro began foreseeing the future, reading his friends' auras, and communicating with loved ones who had crossed over. Extraordinarily gifted, Jethro Smith was intensely tested and mentored by Master Teachers beginning preschool throughout his twenties.

Jethro Smith first public appearance was at age eight when he prophesied to a widow on the steps of a Baptist church.
Not realizing the deceased husband was invisible to others, he admonished the newly-deceased husband for speaking too gruffly to his widow regarding the missing wedding rings. The incident concluded with a large gathering surrounding the widow who was so astonished that she fainted. Jethro Smith is open in all modalities: clairvoyant, clairaudient, telepathic, precognitive, and retrocognitive, and due to the range of his abilities is known for swift, concise, and powerfully accurate readings.

He is sensitive to persons of all walks of life, religions, and countries. Through his unique personal life and experiences from the other side, Jethro has developed a refreshing approach to life and the afterlife. He is nonjudgmental, empathetic, and not easily taken by surprise.

Jethro is an exceptionally accurate reader with a sense of humor attained from the perspective of seeing the larger picture of life's experiences. Jethro is the father of two sons, one having crossed over, and the grandfather of two grandsons. Jethro Smith has professionally served clients for over 30 years, individually and corporately, including: public radio; coalition against violence; prosecution, defense; investigative and criminal discovery.
Jethro is a certified psychic, medium, tarot and palm reader, reiki master, founder and host of the award-winning blog talk radio Psychics Gone Wild and author of Living in the Psychic Realm.

Awards received:
- Ranked 55th in the World by The American Federation of Certified Psychics, Mediums and Lightworkers 2013.
- Recognized in The United States National Register of Tested, Certified and Bona Fide Lightworkers, Psychics and Mediums.
- Listed in The World's Best and Most Trusted Psychics, Mediums and Healers.

Featured in: Covington Who's Who.

Rates/Fees:
- $65.00 for 1/2 hour.
- $125.00 for 1 hour.

Personal message or philosophy: Jethro believes that each person is born with the gift of psychic ability which can be suppressed or which can be further heightened through training or through life's experiences. Just as each person is responsible for their individual life choices, so is each person responsible for how they seek information for personal growth in their life.
Developing one's metaphysical gifts can provide powerful insight to enable a person to make healthy, wise choices. One should always "test the spirits" to ensure they are "staying in the light" in according with one's belief in the Higher Power.

*** *** ***

I believe that the more love we spread more successful we can become.
-*Karina Voroshilova*

Karina Voroshilova
Certified by the American Federation of Certified Psychics and
Mediums. New York.

Contact: Email: mediumkarina@gmail.com
Phone: 847 414 1592

Website: www.karinavoroshilova.com

Specialty: Psychic, medium, tarot, healer, and flower essences
practitioner.

Years of practice/experience: 10 years.

Languages: Russian, English.

Profile: Psychic Readings by Karina are a unique and exciting way to get a glimpse into the future and into your past. Karina's readings are fun, accurate, and extremely revealing. Gifted from birth, she was trained by her Russian Grandmother in the use of intuition and crystal healing. Karina gives excellent insight into love and relationships, career and life direction.
Karina uses a no-nonsense, direct approach which is very quick, grounded and accurate. She takes her work very seriously and provides an authentic service for you which is fast and efficient. In her psychic readings, Karina is not here to simply tell you what you already know, but to help you discover answers to the unknown!

Awards received:
- Best Psychic in the World #15.
- Best Psychic in the USA # 12.
- Best Mediums in the World # 12.
- Best Mediums in the USA # 10.
- Best Astrologist and Numerologist # 66.
- Best Numerologist and Numerologist in the USA # 38.
- Best Healers in the World # 39.
- Best Healers in the USA # 14.
- Best Tarot Readers in the World # 7.
- Best Tarot Readers in the USA # 3.

Featured in: American Psychic & Medium Magazine, Times Press Square.

Rates/Fees: $125.00 for 60 minutes.

Personal message: My message and philosophy I live by and I try to instill in my people. I believe each and every one, is here, to help one another.
I do believe in helping and in standing up for what I believe in, and to help my people stand up for what they believe in and teach them to trust their own intuition.

I believe by getting a psychic reading, we can see what shaped us, into who we are. I see people for who they are , yet I don't judge, we all have to survive and we all have to be strong , but its ok to break down, even the strongest ones do have a hard time in life. God does not judge, nor does he punish.

I believe that the more love we spread more successful we can become and more loving. Appreciate what you have and what is around, the people the beauty outside and most importantly love yourself and take care of your body, mind spirit.
Learn to love yourself first, than you can love others with passion and understanding. Be fearless, fear drives negativity. Appreciate everything good or bad you can learn and see why certain things or situation has happened to you.

*** *** ***

**I believe that a person's level
of acceptance is directly
congruent to their level
of happiness.**
-Reverend Kimberly Ward

Reverend Kimberly Ward

American Federation of Certified Psychics and Mediums. New York.

Contact: newbeginningskim@yahoo.com
Phone: 315-783-6867

Website: www.newbeginningsholisticwellness.com

Specialty: Certified Psychic, Certified Medium, Oracle Card Reader, Shamanic Practitioner, Dream Interpreter, Reiki Master, Level III Integrated Energy Therapist.

Years of practice/experience: 10+

Languages: English

Profile: Kimberly is an awarded Psychic Medium and Dream Interpreter. Born with gifts that were developed later in life. She is Clairvoyant, Clairsentient, Clairaudient and empathic. She taps into the energy of her clients and those around her client(s) to bring messages to assist in finding clarity.
Kimberly continues to study, practice and grow as a Psychic, Medium and Wellness Coach and has clients all over the world.
As a dream specialist Kimberly believes that dreams are a result of something unresolved in your life and interpretation is another means of finding clarity.

Awards received:
- Ranked #3 for Mediums by Times Square Press 2013-2014;
- Ranked #6 for Psychics by Times Square Press 2013-2014

Featured in:
- Bellesprit Magazine;
- American Psychic and Medium Magazine;
- The United States and The World's Best Psychics, Mediums, Healers, Astrologers, Palmists, Witches and Tarot Readers 2013-2014;
- Art, UFOs & Supernatural Magazine.

AMERICAN PSYCHIC & MEDIUM

FEBRUARY 2014

**KIMBERLY WARD
AND THE OCCULT
FACE TO FACE
HOW TO SET UP A SÉANCE**

**WHY SHOULD
WE TRUST
PSYCHICS?**

★★★★★
VOTE
DAVID GEFFEN FOR PRESIDENT
★★★★★

The world of spirits, summoning
entities, communicating with our
dead pets, and the afterlife

**INTERVIEWING AMERICA'S
BEST PSYCHICS & MEDIUMS**

Kimberly Ward on the cover of American Psychic & Medium
Magazine, February 2014 Issue.

126

Rates/Fees:
- Readings $30/15 minutes;
- $50/30 minutes;
- Dreams $25.00.

All other services by request. Available for Private Functions

Personal message: I believe that a person's level of acceptance is directly congruent to their level of happiness.
A lack of acceptance creates a resistance that blocks the ability to live in a state of Joy.

*** *** ***

I know that we wouldn't be able to save
everyone, but if we could touch
a percentage of the population
it would be all about the vibration
being put out.
-Le Vans Figueredo

Le Vans Figueredo
American Federation of Certified Psychics and Mediums. New
York.

Contact: Email: levansfigueredo@gmail.com
Telephone: 951-852-6477
Website: ESPsychics.com/psychics/Levans

Specialty: Psychic, Tarot Card Reader, Certified Life Coach,
Clairaudient, Clairsentient, Clairvoyant.

Years of practice/experience: 15 years plus.

Languages: English and Spanish.

Profile: I can answer questions relating to career, relationships, past lives, and coach you with your own intuition. The tools I use are simply to give me a boost into the realm I am entering. My tools will range from tarot deck(s), numerology, crystals, colored candles and essential oils or aromatherapy suggestions for purposes of serenity and healing.

I enjoy relaying messages in the way that I do because there is a sense of gratification on both sides; the recipient attains an extent of closure and perhaps a sense of healing and for me it is about the release of information stored with in.

I except question(s) by telephone, text, chat or via email.

A majority of my messages come from visions while in a state of meditation and or during a conversation with my recipient or via my dreams. These gifts inherited rum about five (5) generations deep and I give gratitude and thanks every day to my ancestral lineage of psychics, mediums, channelers and shamans for having such natural gifts.

Awards received: I became the first (1st) ESPsychic.com to obtain a FIVE star rating in the following areas: Knowledge, professionalism, accommodating, overall talent, recommend To Others.

Rates/Fees: Negotiable.

Personal message or philosophy: My philosophy is to assist others in a spiritual level and show others that every one is gifted.

I know that we wouldn't be able to save everyone, but if we could touch a percentage of the population it would be all about the vibration being put out.

To be able to show and demonstrate that every person is unique in their gifted intuition they are able to improve their quality of living, if they chose.

As for myself, I would like to be a part of a group that is going in this direction already and is in an ascension process to higher levels of energy and frequency vibrations.

I believe that in groups, or higher number(s) people, we can make a difference by way of quality of life, environmentally, psychologically, and of course spiritually.

**We are divine energies
in our bodies of light.**
-Dr. Linda Salvin

Linda Salvin, PhD

Contact: Email: info@lindasalvin.com
Phone: 818-788-6077

Website: www.famous-psychic.com

Specialty: Psychic, metaphysical healer, parapsychologist, medium, radio talk show host and spiritualist.

Years of practice/experience: 23.

Languages: English.

Profile: Dr. Linda Salvin is one of the original four radio psychics having started on a major FM station in Los Angeles in 1994. Not born psychic, Linda had 3 NDEs starting with a plane crash in 1981 at which time she had an out of body experience, became very psychic and her life changed forever.

Linda has over 19 years as a radio broadcaster, and has helped thousands of people on and off the air spiritually.
Her radio broadcasting career began as the night-time psychic on Los Angeles' KBIG 104-FM. Later she produced and hosted her own show on KIEV 870 AM in Southern California, prior to her move to the Cable Radio Networks.
CRN is a national audio broadcast system carried through the cable TV systems, big dish satellite, and streamed over the internet.
In 2004, she began to syndicate her show "Linda Salvin: Visions & Solutions" nationally to radio stations.
By 2005, Linda was on in Los Angeles' KLSX 97.1 FM Talk and drew between 35-52 callers a night. She was on FM talk for following three years until the station went off the air.
Her psychic, metaphysical healing and channeling abilities are amazing, stunning and very accurate. Thousands of testimonials from the homeless to celebrities are on file. Linda developed the successful candle magic line, Wicks of Wisdom.

As a spiritual health educator, parapsychologist, psychic, healer and medium. She has been seen on TV, in a movie and heard on radio as a host and a guest for over 20 years.

Awards received:
- State of CA, State Assembly Certificate of Recognition for helping people on radio,
- The City of West Covina recognition for supporting the community,
- Be Real Broadcasting award three years in a row for top Psychic Radio Broadcast.
- A Master of Public Health degree was awarded in 1977.
- A PhD in Metaphysics in 2008.

Featured in:
- The Return of Mikey by Diane Bucci,
- Dream Reachers II by Betty Dravis,
- Numerous publications of the American Federation of Certified Psychics & Mediums,
- Several newspaper articles, blogs, etc.

Rates/Fees:
- $149 an hour,
- $79 for 30 minutes.
- Channeling and healings are more.

Dr. Linda Salvin is available by appointment.

Personal message or philosophy: Each of us are divine energies in our bodies of light. We have darkness to overcome and as a lightworker, I have helped over 40,000 people get on their path, find light and God and move forward on their journey.

*** *** ***

**Each client is special
and each session is sacred.**
-Melissa Berman

Melissa Berman
Certified by the American Federation of Certified Psychics and Mediums. New York.

Contact info: Email: mabermanarts@gmail.com
Phone: (Office) 818.994.4488
(Cell) 818.424.4296
Website: amcpm.org

Specialty: Intuitive Spiritual Coach, Psychic and Medium/Channeling and Psychometry.

Years of practice/experience: Over 25 years.

Language: English.

Profile:
Melissa Berman is an internationally recognized intuitive spiritual coach, psychic and medium bringing over 25 years experience in the healing arts field.
Melissa's work includes channeling, psychometry, pendulum and candle reading, and she is clairaudient, clairsentient and clairvoyant.

Each session with Melissa provides nurturing, practical integrity-based guidance for healing and empowerment including nutrition, personal and professional growth, relationships, past lives, astrological aspects, animal communication, meeting spiritual guides and connecting to those who have passed on.
In addition, Melissa continues her extensive work with Indigo, at-risk and children with special needs and their families.
As a teaching artist in theatre/dance/music, Melissa is able to spark imaginations and promote creativity in a safe and joyful environment.
Melissa Berman is also a professional award-winning, critically-acclaimed singer, musician, actress and dancer. As a headlining performer, Melissa has been seen at such noted venues as The Center Theatre (L.A.), The Roxbury (L.A.), Don't Tell Mama (N.Y.), Katie O'Toole's (N.Y.), The John F. Kennedy Center for the Performing Arts, (D.C.) and Blues Alley (D.C.)

Melissa Berman has an extensive background in film, television, commercials and radio with national performing credits working with such noted directors as James L. Brooks and Barry Levinson; featured with NPR and the BBC.

Melissa's vast work includes studying with the late renowned reader Reverend Ernest S. Longest and serving as Executive

Assistant to the President of the esteemed Hay House Publishing Company, Louise L. Hay, Publisher/Owner.

Melissa Berman holds a BFA (honors) in Dramatic Art and Speech and Graduate Work in Educational Theatre from Virginia Commonwealth University. Member of the American Federation of Certified Psychics and Mediums; SAG-AFTRA.

Awards: Performing and teaching awards including the drama-logue critics award.

Featured in: Numerous books and magazines.

Rates/fees: as follows: 15 minutes = $30.00
- 30 minutes = $60.00
- 45 minutes = $90.00
- 60 minutes = $125.00 (a one hour session also includes follow-up questions pertaining to that reading for up to 15 minutes gratis within two weeks of the session.)

Melissa is available for classes, workshops, galleries, events and parties. Rates vary. Contact Melissa for further information.

Personal message: It is a privilege to do this work, and I am very grateful for every opportunity to offer and share my services. Each client is special and each session is sacred.
There is no "quick fix" when it comes to the path unfolding.
There are unlimited ways of discovering, exploring and finding what is right for each individual.

Many possibilities are presented to bring comfort and answers to each client through guidance in a healing arts session. When we follow these prompts, our lives become more meaningful, we begin to really feel and sense and become aware, and thus, more empowered and loving. Although the guidance may not always be what one thinks it ought to be, it has to be respected as sacred information being presented to enhance the journey.

I have been a reader now for over 25 years and a student on the path since I was very young ~ keeping the sacredness, honoring the importance of the guidance and always with devotion to the Divine is what has become clearly to me my mission.

I take it very seriously and with gratitude and humility. It is the driving force of my life, and I am completely devoted 24/7. Every session, each time of connecting with a client is a blessing unto itself. Thank you from my heart to yours.

*** *** ***

**I love merging aspects of
inner and outer transformation.**
-Melissa Stamps

Melissa Stamps

Certified by the American Federation of Certified Psychics and Mediums. New York.

Contact:
info@3rdeyeopennycpsychic.com
Phone: 201-865-3823

Website: 3rdeyeopennycpsychic.com

Specialty: I am a Psychic Medium and Energy Designer who works with different lineages of Energy work. I believe in holistic, intuitive dynamic and transformational approaches to energy work that includes Psychic readings and Spirit contact.
This includes Psychometry, past life regression, Clairvoyance, trance healing. My areas of training and professional experience include Shiatsu, Shamanic bodywork, Hypnotherapy. I am also a professional Interior Designer and Feng Shui practitioner.

Years of practice/experience: I have been in private practice since 2007. I have been creating ways of helping people transform their lives as a Shiatsu practitioner and Energy worker since 1997.

Languages: English and high school French.

Profile: Melissa grew up in New York City.
She is a Clairvoyant, Empath and Energy Worker.
Melissa is also a trained and certified Psychic Medium, and certified Hypnotherapist. She assists clients in re-activating their knowledge using Clairvoyance, Intuition, Energy healing, out of body experiences, work with Color, crystals, hypnosis, past life regression and existences in other star systems.
Melissa loves merging aspects of inner and outer transformation and her Energy work includes experiencing many dimensions at once.
She is a member of the American Association of Psychics and Mediums, and the American Federation of Certified Psychics and Mediums. Other professional organizations include:
The International Feng Shui Guild,
The International Association for Professional Life Coaches.
International Association of Counselors and Therapists.

Melissa is also trained in Shamanic journeying and bodywork, trance healing, Physical and Mental Mediumship and Spirit Release. She lives and works in the New York City area, where she does both telephone readings and in person readings, as well as healings, and mentorships.

Melissa Stamps' lineages are Pre-Minoan, Dianic and Shamanic Goddess mysteries, Melissa is also a successful certified Interior Design stylist and Feng Shui practitioner, and a graduate of the Ohashi Institute of Advanced Shiatsu Studies. Her approach is passionate, energetic, and multi-dimensional. All dimensions of a person's life are explored, seen and worked on energetically for successful transformation. Melissa's expertise shows her clients the benefits of connecting to Spirit and developing a relationship with their Guides to accelerate clarity, awareness, and success. She can awaken a sense of passion and focus, as well as improved health and more energy. Through understanding and connecting to Source, you will reawaken your talents and abilities that lead to infinite possibilities.
Her clients experience intense emotional connection to deeper understandings of their own life as well as messages from loved ones who have crossed into spirit. Sometimes a simple message

will help change feelings of years of grief and create a new sense of hope for the future.

Awards received:
- CHI Award: Feng Shui Award.
- Award of Excellence in Ancestral Healing.

Featured in:
- Magazines: New York Magazine
- Art, UFO's and Supernatural Magazine
- Jersey Journal (Cover Story)
- Books:
- 1.Lightworkers 2013: The Best, The Friendliest: The Certified and The Most Honest.
- 2.Directory & International Rank of the United States and the World's Best Psychics, Mediums, Healers, Astrologers and Lightworkers.
- 3.States Directory & International Rank of the United States and the World's Best Psychics, Mediums, Healers, Astrologers and Lightworkers Volume 2.
- 4.Classement international des meilleurs voyants et mediums en France, Europe, Amerique et dans le monde 2012-2013
- 5.Witchcraft and the Lightworkers Ultimate Techniques to Remove Curses and Stop the Effects of Badmouthing Volume1
- 6.Witchcraft and the Lightworkers Ultimate Techniques to Remove Curses and Stop the Effect of Badmouthing.
- 7. The American Federation of Certified Psychics and Mediums, Official Handbook.
- 8.Register of the United States and World's Best & Most Trusted Psychics, Mediums and Healers in International Rank order 2011-2012.
- 9.America's & World's Best Psychics and Mediums Who Care Most About You.
- 10. 4th edition: Lightworkers of 2012 Hall of Fame of the Most Caring, Lightworkers & World's Best Psychic and Healers Who Care Most About You.
- 11."How to Create a Rich, Successful and Fullfilling Life:

- Dynamic Tools for Overcoming Obstacles and Creating Rapid Transformation" (Co-author).
- 12.Successful Transformation: Expert Life Coaches Share Their Transformational Secrets (Co-author).

Rates/Fees:
- 1 hour: $195;
- ¾ hour: $165;
- ½ hour: $140.

Personal message:
I am drawn to ancient sources and lineages, and the knowledge they transmit from other universes.

Ancient Goddess Mystery from pre-Minoan Crete, Asian Minor, and Shamanic Tibetan.

Advanced information comes from other dimensions through Priestesses, shamans, energy workers and healers, and artists.

This knowledge has become what we know and experience as Clairvoyance, Intuition, energy healing, out of body experiences, work with Color, crystals, hypnosis, past life regression and existences in other star systems.

I assist clients in re-activating their knowledge. I love merging aspects of inner and outer transformation.

Energy work includes experiencing many dimensions at once. When you are connected to Source, the floodgates open. I work with clients at finding their own, as well as cosmic floodgates to create transformation in their lives.

*** *** ***

I've spent my life seeking and learning
the answers I sought as a child,
so as the saying goes,
"Once you learn, you teach".
-Reverend Pamela Beaty

Reverend Pamela Beaty
Certified by the American Federation of Certified Psychics and Mediums. New York.

Contact: Phone: 818. 497. 1950
Email: help@pamelabeaty.net
Website: www.pamelabeaty.net

Specialty: Medium, Past life/Akashic records, Empathic intuitive, Spiritual life coach, Spirit Channeler, and Licensed Minister.

Years of experience: 25 plus.

Languages: English.

Bio: Pamela Beaty is an acclaimed empathic intuitive, medium, spirit channeler, energy healer, licensed minister, and past-life therapist. She is a noted teacher and lecturer in those fields, as well as a writer and published author of "Why am I f'd up? "a spiritual guide to understanding the chaos in your life. Pamela's extraordinary gift has been with her since her early childhood growing up as a minister's kid in Missouri.

She has always had the ability to see and hear spirits, allowing her the opportunity to grow spiritually through the wisdom of enlightened beings.

Her innate intuitive healing ability of "seeing" inside a client's energy system enables her to guide, propel and transform their lives. Her unique talent helps unravel the blocks that challenge us all, whether it is difficulties in relationships, career or the physical body.

She puts the pieces of the puzzle of our complicated lives together, by illuminating any situation, creating the confidence to heal and accelerate moving forward.

Pamela's insight into discovering the source of pain, be it from this lifetime or another, brings about profound transformation, healing and inner peace. As a spirit medium, Pamela has spoken to thousands of spirits on the other side to help bring closure to those family and friends remaining in a body.

The healing potential for those left behind is immeasurable. Along with Pamela's gift of mediumship, she is blessed to have the ability to channel beings that have transcended the earth plane.

With her powerful telepathic gifts, Pamela has also been able to communicate with the Lemurians of Mt. Shasta, Pleiadians, and the Arcuturians, as well as beings from other galaxies.

Pamela's work as an empathic intuitive has helped her clients heal their old wounds, and resolve their unresolved emotions. Her ability to see inside her client's energy system, and listen to the voice of their inner child has given her clients the ability to understand the negative thoughts that block them from happiness.

Being able to also communicate with the subconscious mind gives Pamela the opportunity to explain to her clients the fears that are blocking them from achieving their life purpose. Her capacity for empathy helps her clients heal energetically.

As a past life therapist and Akashic record specialist, Pamela helps her clients better understand the difficulties they are having in relationships with family, friends and work colleagues. Her expertise and knack of accessing the Akashic records gives her clients clarity in their journey on the earth plane. Pamela is able to get to "the source" of anyone's wounds by being able to access the patterns of their soul over all of their lifetimes.

Pamela believes that past life therapy is without a doubt one of the most powerful healing tools available. Pamela's client list runs the gamut from stay at home moms, and business professionals, to celebrity clientele.

She has assisted law enforcement personnel as well as the victim's families' in solving crimes. Pamela has occupied radio waves nationwide, regularly appearing on KLSX 97.1 FM, WOCA 96.7 FM, Sheena Metal Experience, Mother Love Show, The World According to T.J.Mccormack, Haunted Playground, as well as anchoring her own talk show on LA Talk Radio, and currently hosting the "Truth Be Told" radio show on the Mystic Pig Radio Network.

Her Midwest sensibilities lend themselves to her unpretentious and down to earth style.

She realizes the world of spirit can be intimidating and frightening as well as challenging to the skeptics. Her work integrates her forthright, down to earth approach to life, with compassion and clarity. Combined with her ease and humor, she gently lifts the taboo off the metaphysical.

Featured in:
Book: "Why am I f'd up?" a spiritual guide to understanding the chaos in your life.
Magazine: Journal of Longevity, Cover story
Television:
* Bravo's Flipping Out with Jeff Lewis
* SyFy Channel (pilot)
* VH1 Hollywood EX's
  * Dick Clark Production (pilot)
Radio:
* KLSX 97.1 FM
* WOCA 96.7 FM
* Sheena Metal Experience
* On the Couch with Dr. Michelle
* Dave's Good Vibration Station
* Haunted Playground
* The World According to T.J. McCormack

Rates: In person sessions:
* $ 200 for 1 hr phone session.
* $ 150 for ½ hr.

- Phone session: $75

Personal message: "Why are we here? Why is there so much suffering on Earth? Who is God? Are we alone in the Universe? Who are my ostensible imaginary friends?
These are just a few of the questions I asked as a child.
As a preachers kid, I just did not believe what my father was telling me that God was a punishing, angry father that did not allow mistakes.
I didn't believe for a second that the same God that created the beauty of planet Earth, the animal kingdom, and the human body, could possibly be angry.
I feel so blessed that my fathers beliefs were completely the opposite of mine, because that's what led me to being a seeker of truth. I would never have discovered my abilities as a medium, empathic healer, channeler, or past life therapist had my father not been my nemesis. He gave me a great gift! My journey was to discover the reality of and purpose to life. Discovering the truth has helped me to cope with living in a world where rape, murder, war, theft and dishonesty runs rampant.

While seeking, I started uncovering the truth behind the illusion of suffering. My goal is to help as many people as possible to understand the reasons why their lives are so difficult. I believe that knowledge is power and I want to be the teacher of mental, emotional, and spiritual knowledge. Every human being has problems. The reason I both wrote my book and have a passion for my work, is I get to help people understand those problems. Understanding releases judgment. I've spent my life seeking and learning the answers I sought as a child, so as the saying goes, "Once you learn, you teach".

*** *** ***

I believe that magic is all around us.
-Patti Negri

Patti Negri

Sr. Vice President of the American Federation of Certified
Psychics & Mediums
Chief Examiner of the American Federation of Certified Psychics
and Mediums
Syndicated Columnist.
Hollywood Bureau Chief for Stars Illustrated and APM Magazine

Contact: Phone 323.461.0640
Email Patti@PattiNegri.com

Website: www.PattiNegri.com

Specialty: Psychic, Medium, "Good" Witch, Life Coach, Energy
Healer, Tarot Card Reader Clairvoyant, Empath, Spells, Rituals,
Custom Oils, Clearings, Séances, Magick, Teaching, Lecturing.

Years of practice/experience: 25 years.

Languages: English.

Bio: Patti is a psychic-medium and "good" witch. She was voted
number one Psychic in the US and number one Medium, Tarot
Reader and Witch / Magickal Practitioner in the World for 2013 -
2014.
Patti's working style is magical, loving and upbeat -- which
creates a positive, safe and fun environment for you to learn,
grow and heal.
She has recently graced 5 magazine covers including:
American Psychic & Medium Magazine.
Art, UFO and Supernatural Magazine.
Parapsychology and Mind Power Magazine.
Extraterrestrials Magazine.
Stars Illustrated Magazine.
And contributed or been a part of over 20 books, several of which
are Amazon Bestsellers. Patti is honored to be considered one of
the best psychics in LA, the US and around the world as evident
by her winning these awards for the past 3 consecutive years. She
has been able to communicate with the spirit world since she was
a toddler and consciously since she conducted her first séance at
the age of eight in her childhood home.

Since then she has conducted séances and contacted spirits on radio, film, TV and in living rooms and board rooms across America. Patti has been practicing natural magick her entire life. Her specialty is in adjusting energy and flow – in people, spaces, situations, most anything.

She works organically by creating spells and rituals that arrange natural elements to the rhythms and cycles of the universe. This can bring about healing, change our lives for the better, and create balance.

She has a life-affirming, earth and nature-oriented belief system that honors the natural world as the embodiment of divinity. Patti enjoys working her magic in the realm of television. Patti's recent "other-worldy" television appearances include Jeff Lewis's Flipping Out, some magickal cooking on this seasons Master Chef with Gordon Ramsey, conjuring up a few "dead celebrities" on an episode of Private Chefs of Beverly Hills, an episode of Death Dealers, several episodes of Pit Boss where she performed a "house cleansing" for Shorty and his crew and cleared out the "negative energy" at Shortywood and Beverly Hills Pawn.

She was brought in as a paranormal expert on Ghostly Lovers. She has even gotten into the home makeover world by doing a séance as part of a home renovation on Mobile Home Disaster. In addition to her own Radio Show, Patti has been heard on national syndicated radio with Adam Corolla, Jason Ellis and Mancow Muller.

As a performer Patti has enjoyed numerous stage, film, and television roles, and has had the honor of working with such actors as Martin Sheen, Burt Reynolds, Jon Voight, Chevy Chase and Sylvester Stallone.

She has danced with Gregory Hines, choreographed for David Hasselhoff, cooked for Gordon Ramsey and entertained celebrities on scavenger hunts, photo safari's and toga mysteries across the Greek Islands.

As a producer, Patti owns Brain Brew Entertainment, a boutique theatrical production company that specializes in live interactive entertainment.

She has created shows for clients as diverse as major casinos in Las Vegas to the corporate world of Microsoft and Mattel.

A big believer in thinking globally and acting locally, Patti is committed to helping her planet from the ground up.

She is a community activist, serves on the board of 5 nonprofits. Patti is happily married to the fabulous drummer Kerry Crutchfield, and proud "mom" to pup star Dora.

Testimonials:
Patti is in tune and is the real deal. Her laugh is contagious! Patti has helped cleanse my home and also given me insight into many things about myself. I called Patti and just asked for a home cleansing and still was a bit skeptical....Without telling her where I kept seeing this "being" Patti showed up and immediately walked into the hallway where I would see this thing and called it out. She helped cleanse, and also do some "chord cutting." It's amazing the spiritual journeys that Patti has taken me to and it's both psychologically and spiritually healing!!!!! There are a lot of energy workers/psychics that basically do the psychology readings or are just empaths, but Patti does the truth and is the real deal...

She's also a very warm comforting person to be around and is very trustworthy... She'll definitely open your eyes to new things that have always been and makes it so simple for you to understand and she connects with the soul...

Patti is an intuitive psychic who helps guide people toward all that is positive. She blessed my new home and cleared out the negative energy from the previous owners.

She always works toward hers and her clients' highest good and greatest joy. I have known Patti for over 25 years. She has an extraordinary gift that I have seen her use to help many people. Patti is so full of love and compassion for the human plight and this makes it so easy to talk to her. Her advice and observations are right on.

Patti Negri is ethical, compassionate and is willing to go the extra mile with a person (both in the physical and psychic realm). She is supportive of others and their development of talents and gifts. Patti, supports others through her knowledge and ethical psychic talents!

Patti is generous, kind, and perpetually bubbly individual, she takes her work very seriously and constantly applies herself. She's an inspiration! So, what more could one ask for?

Just wanted to drop you a line regarding the influence Patti Negri has had on my life. I lost my Father and my Husband within a week of each other over a year ago. I was beside myself. I turned to Patti Negri for some spiritual advice.

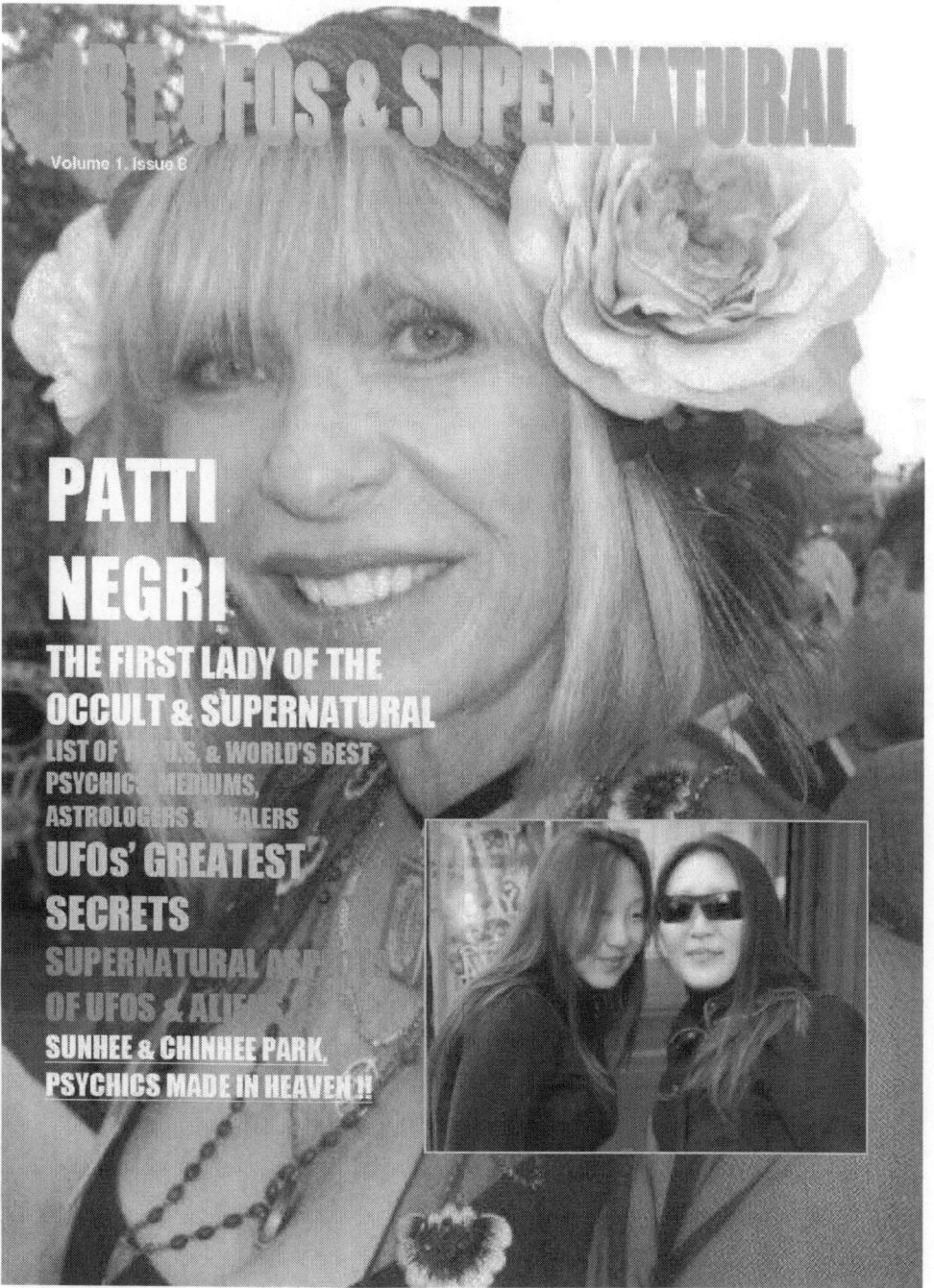

Patti Negri on the cover of Art, UFOs & Supernatural Magazine.

Patti was so insightful regarding how she was able to comfort me. She was so knowledgeable with matters of the other side. She gave me peace of mind with her ability to communicate with my dearly departed love ones. It wasn't an easy task for her, but she was determined to help me understand that all was well for my dear Father and Husband.

She also sensed that the house was very sad and gave it a spiritual cleansing that has made all the difference with the way my sons and I feel living here now.

She was amazing and I can only say that without her expertise, I would have had a very difficult time with their unexpected departure. Thank goodness Patti was there for me!

Patti is a "guide" to me, of sorts, by virtue of her open heart, generous spirit and intuitive gifts. She has tremendously helped me in awakening my consciousness and has been very supportive of my own healing practice.

Awards received:
- Voted # 1 Psychic in the U.S. for 2013-2014
- Voted #1 Medium in the World for 2013-2014
- Voted #1 Tarot Reader in the World for 2103-2014
- Voted #1 Witch / Magickal Practitioner in the World for 2013 – 2014
- Top Psychic & Medium Awards last 3 consecutive years
- Tested & Certified Psychic Medium   AMCPM.org

Featured in:
- Patti has recently graced 5 magazine covers including American Psychic & Medium Magazine, Art, UFO and Supernatural Magazine, Parapsychology and Mind Power Magazine, Extraterrestrials Magazine and Stars Illustrated Magazine, and has contributed or been a part of over 20 published books, several of which are Amazon Bestsellers.
- Partial List of Books:
- Lightworkers 2013: The Best, The Friendliest: The Certified and The Most Honest.
- Directory & International Rank of the United States and the World's Best Psychics, Mediums, Healers, Astrologers & Lightworkers.

- United States Directory & International Rank of the United States and the World's Best Psychics, Mediums, Healers, Astrologers & Lightworkers.
- Classement international des meilleurs voyants et mediums en France, Europe, Amerique et dans le monde 2012-2013.
- Witchcraft and the Lightworkers Ultimate Techniques to Remove Curses and Stop the Effects of Badmouthing Volumes 1, 2.
- The American Federation of Certified Psychics and Mediums, Official Handbook.
- Register of the United States and World's Best & Most Trusted Psychics, Mediums and Healers in International Rank order 2011-2012.
- America's & World's Best Psychics and Mediums Who Care Most About You.
- 4th edition: Lightworkers of 2012 Hall of Fame of the Most Caring, Lightworkers & World's Best Psychic and Healers Who Care Most About You.
- The United States and the World's Best Psychics, Mediums, Healers, Astrologers, Palmists, Witches and Tarot Readers 2013-2014.

Rates/Fees:
Regular readings or sessions:
- $120.00 for 60 minutes.
- $90.00 for 45 minutes.
- $60.00 for 30 minutes.
- Sessions can be in person, by phone or skype.

Patti is based in Hollywood California and offers House and Office Clearings and Blessings, Séances, Private Parties, Galleries, Workshops and Lectures in local Southern California area –and is also available for travel nationally and internationally. Call for pricing and details.

Personal message:
My working style is magical, loving and upbeat, which creates a positive, safe and fun environment for you to learn, grow and heal. I believe that magic is all around us.

I do not believe that you have to be a witch or a psychic to empower your life and create true change. My goal is to use my psychic and medium gifts to guide, help and empower YOU to take charge and create the life you want.

I work with mother earth's natural elements, using oils, herbs, sounds and stones in many of my workings. My philosophy in no way clashes with any spiritual or religious beliefs because magic is energy based and works within all belief systems. Psychics, Mediums, and Lightworkers have always had a challenge to get the respect they need.

Unfortunately that is understandable, since for every real and bona fide psychic, there is one that is a fake, charlatan or scam artist.

That is why the Federation of Certified Psychics and Mediums was created. We wanted to "raise the bar" on professionalism in our field.

We wanted to give the public a real, valid and dependable place to find legitimate, honest and ethical lightworkers.

The Federation is a 501 c3 not for profit organization that is made up of the best of the best of lightworkers worldwide. Every psychic who wants to be a member has to be tested and certified. Even legitimate lightworkers and practitioners with years of practice and documented accomplishments have to be tested to adhere to our high standards.

A certification clearly identifies the member as someone who has demonstrated a mastery of certain skills. Our certification clearly discloses the details of the practitioners' expertise, their rates, refund policies and specialties, providing confidence and information for clients.

If you are looking for the best in psychics, mediums, healers and lightworkers, you will find them at the American Federation of Certified Psychics and Mediums! Go to our website for profiles and information on each of our members.

www.americanfederationofcertifiedpsychicsandmediums.org
www.amcpm.org

*** *** ***

160

Faith, Courage and Love is Key.
-Reverend Robert M. Rodriguez

Rev. Robert Madrid Rodriguez
Certified by the American Federation of Certified Psychics and
Mediums. New York.

Contact: email: robert.m.rodriguez@me.com;
whitewolfhealer333@gmail.com,
Phone: (310)701-6830, etc.
Website: www.facebook.com/psychicmediumrobert

Specialty: Intuitive Psychic Medium, Tarot Cards, Tea Leaf,
Clairvoyant, Claraudient, Clarsentient, Empathic, Scrying,
Remote Viewing, Energy Healing, Spiritual Healing, ET
Channeling, Aura Reading, Medical Body Scanning, Spiritual
Magic, Carribean magick, Shaman, Candle Magick, Incense,
Mantras, Hinduism, Budism, Meditations, Guided Meditations,

Sanskrit Mantras, Spiritual Oils, Enochian Magick, Working with angels & spirit guides, European magick, Latin magick. All Magic performed is within the light.

Years of practice/experience: I have had 24 years of experience as an Intuitive Psychic Medium and Practicing Spiritual/Shamanic/Magical Practitioner.

My experience began at the young of 7, where at this time I was able to speak with people whom have crossed over to the other side, was able to read people, as well as foresee things before they occurred. I was also taught from a very young age how to work with magic on so many different levels and forums, as I am a 5th generation Psychic Medium and Magical Practitioner, also as I have had the blessing and privilege of studying under some of the worlds most well respected Shamans, Magical Practitioners, and Intuitive Psychic Mediums.

Languages: English and Spanish, and speaks Sanskrit (mantra purposes).

Profile: Robert is a born intuitive psychic medium, whom first discovered his gifts at the age of 6 yrs and began using them at 7 yrs of age. He is 5th generation in his family to have such gifts. His family has come from a long line of psychics, healers, shamans and magical practitioners. Since Robert has begun his spiritual journey he has found that his spirit has taken him down many different avenues of the metaphysical plane, where he has been blessed to have studied with some of the worlds best Magical, Spiritual & Psychic practitioners.

Robert believes his gifts came from God and works to aid others, in hopes that they will find the joy, peace and love in life that he has, through his readings, healings, magick, and teachings. Robert is also an Ordained Minister and proud member of the Nationally Certified Psychics and Mediums organization. He has been featured in radio shows, magazines, spiritual conventions, and has hosted his own psychic & medium galleries, etc. Robert is not only Psychic he is also a energetic/spiritual healer, magical practitioner and Shaman.

He has studied Hinduism, Buddhism, candle magic, Caribbean magic, European magick, Shamanistic magic, Italian magick, meditations of all levels including guided meditations and has now integrated Reiki and Tai Chi.

Robert believes in working solely with his spirit guides, ancestors and angels in the light to help bring forth a very clear, healing, and insightful message to all those whom seek his help. Robert has chosen to use his God given gifts to aid others as he feels that this is one of his major sole purposes in life. Robert believes that everyone needs guidance in life during troubles, confusions, heartache, etc, which is why he has devoted himself to helping others in their time of need through the use of his gifts, healings and magic.

Featured in:
- American Psychic & Medium magazine since June of 2012 and was on the cover in October 2012.
- Featured on Psychics Gone Wild
- Be the Light Now radio shows.

Rates/Fees:
- $30 for an intuitive reading,
- $40.00 for Medium reading,
- $50 for both an Intuitive & Medium reading,
- $10-20 for candle magic, mantras, prayers,
- Healings are free.

Personal message: God gives his hardest battles to his strongest children. Faith, Courage and Love is Key. You never know which door will lead you towards your dreams, until you have the courage and faith to walk through it.

**Changing your life
is only a decision away.**
-Shannon Leischner

Shannon Leischner
Certified by the American Federation of Certified Psychics and Mediums. New York.

Contact: shannonleischner@yahoo.com
Phone: 1888-SHE-KNOWS

Website: www.shannonleischner.com

Specialty: Psychic, medium, motivational speaker, energy healer, Theta healer/instructor, angel communicator, life path coach, spiritual counselor, tarot reader.

Years of practice/experience: 20 years.

Languages: Spanish and English.

Profile: Shannon Leischner is world renowned psychic medium and Theta Healer/Instructor who was born with powerful inherited abilities from generations of truly gifted family members.

For over 20 years, she's been providing psychic readings through her mediumship and empathetic abilities in order to help people from all over the world find their life path and deeper relationships with their higher source.

Shannon Leischner has an extraordinary ability to communicate, interact, and cross over entities that are in the spiritual realm.

Along with her metaphysical training, Shannon also has an MPA in Public Administration.

All services are provided with caring, insight and discretion.

Recently, Shannon was featured in Psychic 4 U Psychic News, Views, and Interviews (an online magazine). She has been a guest psychic on "Let Us Connect", Darkness Radio, Kim Iverson, Be The Light Now, No Ordinary Psychic Radio, Queen Mary, Paranormal Radio, Country Music Awards Gala, Media Madness Event, and will soon make her debut on several HBO programs.

Featured in numerous books and magazines.

Rates/Fees:
- 15 minutes $65
- 30 minutes $95
- 1 hour $175

Personal: Changing your life is only a decision away. Make the decision to give and attract love and positive energy in your life and you will see your life transform.

***   ***   ***

I hope to bring you clarity and happiness.
-Sherie Roufosse

Sherie Roufosse
Certified by the American Federation of Certified Psychics and
Mediums. New York.

Contact: Email tay-yay@hotmail.com

Website: mediumsherie.com

Specialties: Psychic, medium.

Years of experience: 20

Languages: English.

Profile: Descendant of generations of highly gifted mediums and psychics. Born with the psychic gifts of smelling, hearing, feeling, and seeing.

For me, signals come in different forms via one of these senses, or even a photographic image in my mind. From the age of 2 I have memories of hiding under my baby brothers crib when spirits came.

As I grew up, I learned not to fear them, but ask them what they needed, or, if they were here to help me.

I have learned to understand the gift of clarity that has been bestowed on me, as the spirits show me many things.

Rates:
- Email reading $25.
- Phone, chat or skype $30 for 30 minutes
- Phone, chat or skype $150 for 60 minutes.

Personal message: We are all made up of energies, always changing to what we need. We do this by changing how we think, act, education, experiences, the people who pass through our lives, what we accept, what we consciously and unconsciously accept.

Our belief systems change according to our experiences and learning. By using our thought process, and taking actions we can manifest what we want and or what is needed. Keeping in mind energy can work for or against us.

Keeping grounded and tapped into the energies around us help and guide us through life. Opening to the positive energies: Angels, guides and protection with the higher positive benefits clarity.

If you choose to stay asleep,
then you are missing out on
the wonderful world of the unknown.
-Sunhee Park

Sunhee Park

Certified by the American Federation of Certified Psychics and Mediums. New York.

Contact: Sunhee@ESPsychics.com
Phone: 347-826-1425,
Website:
http://espsychics.com/psychics/sunhee-park/

Specialty: Psychic, medium, Energy healer, ET channeler, Psychometry, Clairaudient, ESP.

Years of practice/experience: 15

Languages: English, semi fluent in Spanish

Profile: Both Chinhee and Sunhee recognized their gifts of clairvoyance, empathy, telepathy, and mediumship at a young age. At 15, they both had the same dream of their mother dying from Cancer.
Their prediction came true shortly after. At 19, the twins started to exercise more of their abilities within the entertainment industry. It was during this time that they were spotted in the streets of Manhattan by an NBA basketball player and talent agent.
This talent agent sent them on auditions for small parts in Law & Order, MTV, TBS, Independent Films as psychics, Estee Lauder Shoot, Got Milk Twins, Marie Claire Magazine, Book of Twins, Time, People, and many other international magazines and newspapers. That was an amazing experience for these two small town girls.
This leads to finding themselves taking an interest in what was taking place behind the scenes and as a result soon took over their agent's business. This agent was amazed at their ability to know what actors or models were going to get booked for a specific project. At 21, they were considered the youngest talent managers in the industry and the only company who specialized with "ethnic" and "real" people.

172

The twins also worked for a boutique business management firm that represented A-list celebrities such as Raquel Welch, Judy Collins, NBA Basketball Stars, actors/models/artists.

They also did aerial photography by hanging out of a Robinson R22 helicopter without a door.

They shot riots, celebrity weddings, news coverage, the O.J. case and so on.

Sunhee worked with NY-1 News assisting the Celebrity reporter for high society events, and movie premieres while Chinhee was at Paramount Pictures helping Don Johnson in casting his t.v. series.

Their path took them to where they are today in the spiritual world. In 2010, the Park twin-sisters hosted their own radio show on CBS for over 2 years. Apart from hosting a show, they have also been guests on Mothership Radio, LA Talk, various CBS radio shows, and several others.

In 2010, the twins were invited to offer their gifts for the 2011 Feb. Grammy Award presenters and nominees. Their certificates will be placed in the SWAG bags for Celine Dion, Kelly Preston, and Mariah Carey's baskets. All thanks to HollywoodBaskets.com owned by Lisa Gal Bianchi.

Awards received:
- 2012: Voted # 1 Best Psychic in the U.S. with Patti Negri.
- Voted #3 Best Psychic in the World.
- 2012: Voted #3 by for the International Register of the United States for Best Psychics.
- 2012: Voted as one of "The Most Caring Psychics in the World".
- 2012: Voted as one of the top 5 Best Psychics and Mediums in the world, UFO's and Supernatural Magazine, issue 5.
- 2012: Appointed Chief Examiners of The American Federation Of Certified Psychics & Mediums (AFCPM).
- Certified Psychic and Mediums by AFCPM.
- 2011: Sunhee made top 12 Psychic in the world in "The Battle of The Psychics" television show in the Ukraine. She declined the contract to do her own television show in the states with her sister.

Featured in:

- The United States and the World's Best Psychics, Mediums, Healers, Astrologers, Palmists, Witches and Tarot Readers 2013-2014
- Cover of the book: "International Register for the World's Best Psychics, Mediums, Astrologer, Light Workers. Volume II. In addition, Graced the cover of the French version of this book.
- Graced the cover of "Art, UFO & Supernatural" Magazine, 2012, with fellow psychic Patti
- Graced the cover and feature story of the book "International Register of the United States for Best Psychics."
- 2012: Graced the cover of Bellesprit magazine.
- 2012: A new book about "Bullying" by Jill Vanderwood.

Rates/Fees: $225.00/hr.
Discount for first time clients

Personal message: I believe that we all are shifting faster and have no choice to wake up. If you choose to stay asleep, then you are missing out on the wonderful world of the unknown. Just because you cannot touch it does not mean it does not exist. Get in tune with yourself and accept that you are special!

*** *** ***

Believe in 'unity consciousness'.
-Sunanda Sharma

Sunanda Sharma

Contact: email - sunandasharma2011@gmail.com
Phone- +91 9808125113 (India)

Website: www.sunandatarot.com

Specialty: Psychic, tarot, spiritual counselor, reiki healer, life coach, author.

Years of practice/experience: 10yrs +

Languages: English and Hindi.

Profile: Sunanda Sharma is the author of the book "Inspiration From The Spirit" Vol 1 and Vol 2. She has been offered shows by Sahara TV and has done many Tarot Reading Events. Sunandra Sharma is on the panel of Celestial Corner as a Tarot Expert (celestialcorner.com).

Featured in: World's best psychics, mediums, tarot readers, 2013

Awards received:
- Sunanda is ranked no-3 in the world amongst the category of 'best tarot reader's' in the world.
- Recipient of Lightworkers' World Hall of Fame,
- Recipient of Lightworkers' Life Achievement Award 2013,
- Honoured by www.timessquarepress.com.
- Recipient of "Tarot Super Achiever's Award - 2012" for Tarot Diva's in India conferred by NGO Bharat Nirman.
- Winner of 'Super Achievers Award 2013' for 'Spiritual Counseling' by NGO Bharat Nirman.
- Also an International Felicitation.
- Recipient of the Universal Humanity Award 2013 - awarded by "The International Court of Governors"; appreciations by Women International Network (WIN), Astitv mujhse meri pehchan, Indira Gandhi Technological and Medical Sciences, University of Arunachal Pradesh, The Global University Nagaland and South African High Commission

Rates/Fees: $60, refer to website : www.sunandatarot.com

Personal message: Believe in 'unity consciousness', 'live your dreams- make it big', live in the here and now! Live and let live, unconditional love is the flavour of life.

***   ***   ***

**My goal is to touch as many
people as I possibly can,
every day.
-Suzanne Grace**

Suzanne Grace

Certified by the American Federation of Certified Psychics and Mediums. New York.

Contact: sgracemedium@gmail.com
Phone: 805-341-0388
Website: www.suzannegracemedium.com

Specialty: Psychic, medium, empath and healer with specialty in connecting with loved ones who have crossed over.
Able to connect with the energy of those around the client. Theta healer, Reconnective Healer, Reiki as well as Certified Angel Practitioner.

Years of practice/experience: 16.

Languages: English.

Profile: As a young girl Suzanne discovered that she was a psychic medium when she saw her first spirit wandering around her bedroom. She was just 4 years old. Later she learned that she comes from a long line of mediums; she was raised to believe it was a secret and not a gift and it wasn't until about 16 years ago that she went on to give readings and mentor with the likes of James Van Praagh, Rebecca Rosen, and Charles Virtue.
She has ventured into the Paranormal as well, assisting in police investigations as well as families with "visitors" who are no longer welcome.
She assists the family in sending the spirit home.
She co-founded a business, The Trinity Paranormal Resolution Services and can often be found assisting families with resolving spiritual and paranormal concerns within their homes as well as their businesses. Suzanne can read using her guides, the guides of the individual, the loved ones of those who have crossed over as well as using angel cards and other divination tools. She is also highly empathic and tends to feel her client's needs prior to even beginning the reading (sometimes days before). Suzanne is currently finishing her degree in Social and Criminal Justice and is heading to law school in Spring 2014 where her goal is to advocate for the juvenile justice system. As a highly successful real estate agent, she is very passionate about all of her business ventures!

Featured in: American Psychic & Medium, Feb 2014 Issue; In 2014 Suzanne was listed in "The United States and the World's Best Psychics, Mediums, Healers, Astrologers, Palmists, Witches and Tarot Leaders 2013-2014"

In 2012 Suzanne was honored to appear on the cover of "The Register of the United States and World Best & Most Trusted Psychics, Mediums and Healers in International Rank Order 2012," "America & world best psychics & healers who care most about you. (Hall of Fame of the Most Caring Lightworkers)" and "Special edition with an addendum. Volume 1: Directory & international rank of the United States & the world's best psychics, mediums, healers, astrologers, and lightworkers (Best lightworkers of our time)"

Awards:
- Ranked #15 in the world's most popular medium category, 2012.
- Ranked #21 best and most trusted psychic category, 2012.
- Ranked #5 in the world in the category of Psychic, 2013.
- Ranked #4 in the world in the category of Medium, 2013.

Rates/Fees:
- $165/hour.
- $90/half hour.
- $50/15 minutes (offer specials through the year as well); these rates are for via in person, phone or email.
- $50 angel card reading via phone or email.
- Paranormal cleansing: negotiated rate.
- Spiritual Counseling: $165/hour.
- Healing: $165/hour.
- Public appearances and parties/events on negotiated rate.

Personal message: My personal philosophy has always been to pay it forward. God/Creator asked me to do the work that I do which I love and as such my goal is to touch as many people as I possibly can, every day.

By doing so I hope to bring love, joy, peace and hope to others.

**Awareness
is the key.**
-Van Doren Figueredo

Van Doren Figueredo
Certified by the American Federation of Certified Psychics and
Mediums. New York.

Contact: vandorenfigueredo@gmail.com

Phone: (800) 874-4590
Website: www.artistic-in2ition.com

Specialty: Psychic, Tarot Card Reader, Medium, ET Channeler.

Years of Practice: 17 years' experience.

Languages: English and Spanish.

Bio Profile: As a native Californian and coming from a Latino family I have known about my gifts since the age of 10, when I wanted to become a psychologist.
Growing up with a religious background and minister's daughter did not allow me to expand my talent. I knew things before they happened and would see things as visions and in dreams.
My gifts became enhanced after my divorce I was able to see more clearly due to this. I then decided to exercise them with Tarot Cards, Psychic Readings and Mediumship.
I've helped many people from family to friends for approximately 10 years for free.
I now have my own website and do readings professionally and I'm also certified and work with ESPsychics.com.
Most of all my life experiences have helped develop my gifts with a higher vibration. I've been the first in a family of 6 generations who carry this gift and have come out publicly to help others.

Award Received: Certification of Recognition from the American Federation Of Certified Psychics And Mediums.

Featured in:
- Directory & International Rank of The United States & The World's Best Psychics, Mediums, Healers, Astrologers & Lightworkers Volume II
- Parapsychology & Mind Power Volume 1. Issue 1
- Art, UFO's & Supernatural Volume 2, Issue 1
- American Psychic Volume1, Issue 1
- Lightworkers 2013: The Best, The friendliest, The Certified & The Most Honest

Rates:
- $ 80 ½ hour.

- $150 hour Phone Reading.
- Chats and email readings vary in price.
- Mobile Service Available.

Personal Message: I encourage anyone that feels they are different or knows they have a gifted talent to learn how to expand it by educating yourself and building confidence.
We all have the intuitive ability; it's up to you to choose how you will make a difference in a positive way to others and our world today become a better place. Awareness is the key.

*** *** ***

The American Federation of Certified Psychics and Mediums Incorporated, New York
www.amcpm.org

OF CERTIFIED PSYCHICS
AMERICAN FEDERATION
AND MEDIUMS INC
NEW YORK, USA

Legal Status

The American Federation of Certified Psychics and Mediums Incorporated is an official not-for-profit corporation organized and incorporated under the laws of the State of New York, in March 2012. It is the first and only organization of its kind to be state registered and its Articles of Incorporation state approved, in the USA.

The Federation is a state registered corporation with the New York State Department of State/Non-Profit Corporations Division, and as defined in subparagraph (a) (5) of Section 102 of the Not-for-Profit Corporation Law and Section 404 of the Not-For-Profit Corporation Law.

The Federation is organized as a New York Domestic Not-for-Profit corporation. It is organized exclusively for the purposes of developing, recognizing, certifying, and promoting the quality work of psychics mediums, healers, and lightworkers via orientation programs, training, forums, discussions and public awareness.

The Purposes of the Federation are:

- 1-To promote the quality work of psychics, mediums, healers and lightworkers.
- 2-To develop and to enhance the abilities, talents and full potentials of legitimate practitioners in the field.
- 3-To develop, conduct and offer training programs, orientation programs, and professional materials for the better advancement of psychics, mediums, healers, spiritual advisors, lightworkers and their profession.
- 4-To grant official recognition and certifications for qualified practitioners in the field.
- 5-The public objective of the Federation is to help practitioners in the field explore and develop their full potentials and skills, and ameliorate their talents and gifts at no cost to them, and which without the help of the corporation, their work would and could not be acknowledged, made known and appreciated by the public.

Members' Benefits and Privileges
All members are entitled to:

- 1-Receive the Federation's national recognition, recommendation, and full endorsement.
- 2-Receive the Federation's national certification, certificates and diplomas if applicable, or a statement in lieu.
- 3-Be listed free of charge, in the National Directories of Certified and/or Tested Practitioners.

- 4-Be free of charge, featured, and/or written up or interviewed in the Federation's publications, books and affiliated magazines.
- 5-Free of charge Nationwide and worldwide promotion via the Federation's newswire, press releases, and interviews in the Federation's publications.
- 6-Enroll free of charge in the Orientation and Training programs.
- 7-Free of charge National and worldwide maximum exposure provided by the best-selling magazines "American Psychic & Medium Magazine", and "UFOs & Supernatural Magazine". All members will be featured in the magazines on a regular basis, and will have the opportunity to appear on the cover of the magazines.
- 8-Receive free of charge assistance in writing their resumes, CVs, and press releases.
- 9-Have a personal profile (Mini website) on the Federation's website free of charge.
- 10-Receive free of charge review of their published books in the Federation's publications, and magazines.

*** *** ***

A brief note about the author's activities in the paranormal and occult Disciplines

Maximillien de Lafayette's interest in and involvement with the paranormal and metaphysics began in 1953. Although he is a lawyer (Practicing international law and intellectual property law abroad), the author of more than 1,500 books in 26 languages, a linguist and a conservative historian by trade, and thus, a pragmatic thinker, Maximillien's intense fascination by the occult and supernatural phenomena took him on a legendary journey to the realms of the Mounawariin (Enlightened Masters), the Rouhaniyiin (The Spirituals), and Tahiriin (The Pure Ones), known to us as the Honorable Anunnaki Ulema.

Maximillien de Lafayette's was spiritually adopted and taught by the Anunnaki-Ulema in their Ma'haad (School/Center/Temple) and on the roads of enlightenment, they chose to guide him toward Tanwir, and develop his metaphysical abilities in numerous parts of the world, starting from France and Germany to India, Burma, the Himalayas, Ethiopia, Egypt and the Middle East. He received his basic training from, and was initiated by the Honorable Master Mordachai ben Zvi, the Honorable Grand Master Li, and spiritual guides of Les Peres du Triangle, and the Ramadosh Jami'yah.
He studied and taught the occult and the supernatural-psychic Dirasaat (Studies) and Kiraat (Lectures, Teachings) of the Ulema for almost fifty years.
This integral and deeply rooted metaphysical studies, training and experiments gave birth to approximately 250 philosophical, spiritual and metaphysical books and numerous encyclopedias he wrote and made available to seekers, teachers and students around the globe; to name a few (Available at Barnes and Noble, amazon, lulu.com , and thousands of booksellers and distributors around the globe):

From his most recent published books (Bestsellers):
19th Edition. The Book of Ramadosh: 13 Anunnaki Ulema Techniques To Live Longer, Happier, Healthier, Wealthier".

When Heaven Calls You: Connection with the Afterlife, Spirits, 4th Dimension, 5th Dimension, Astral Body, Parallel Dimensions and the Future.

How to Learn the Languages of the Spirits, Ghosts, Angels, Afrit, Djinns, Demons and Entities and Converse with Them

Encyclopedic Dictionary of Spirits' Languages and Lightworkers' Terminology and Secrets you Never Knew

Psychics-mediums' spirits séances and witchcraft: Roster of spirits, angels & demons and how to communicate with them

How To Become An Effective Energy Healer And Master Of The Healing Touch

How to Become an Enlightened Psychic Detective and Remote Viewer: Ulema Psychometry Lessons, Training & Techniques to locate Missing People and Identifying Places & Objects

How to Become an Enlightened Tarot Psychic Reader and Foresee the Future

How to Become an Enlightened Psychic, Medium and Metaphysical Master

America & world best psychics & healers who care most about you: names, profiles, services, contact. (Hall of Fame of the Most Caring Lightworkers)

How to Use Your Mind Power to do the Impossible: How to Positively Change your Future

How to Read Peoples' Vibes and Know Who They Really Are Just by Looking at Them (See their Aura, Sense their Vibes, Feel their Energy

Calendar of Hours & Days Which Bring You Bad Luck & Good Luck: How to Positively Change your Future

Instructions and Techniques for Commanding Spirits and Communicating with Angels and Entities

Anunnaki Ulema Techniques and Tarot Deck To See Your Future. (The world's most powerful book on the occult and foreseeing your future on Earth and in other dimensions)

The essential Maximillien de Lafayette: The Official Anunnaki Ulema Textbook for the Teacher and the Student.

The Anunnaki Ulema Book of Enlightenment: Metaphysical study of the path of wisdom and esoteric knowledge.

In early 2012, Maximillien de Lafayette created the American Federation of Certified Psychics and Mediums Inc., which is incorporated under the Laws of the State of New York.

The Federation is a state registered corporation with the New York State Department of State/Non-Profit Corporations Division, and as defined in subparagraph (a) (5) of Section 102 of the Not-for-Profit Corporation Law and Section 404 of the Not-For-Profit Corporation Law. The Federation is organized as a New York Domestic Not-for-Profit corporation.

The Federation is organized exclusively for the purposes of developing, recognizing, certifying, and promoting the quality work of psychics, mediums, healers, and lightworkers via orientation programs, training, forums, discussions and public awareness.

De Lafayette has to his credits more than 250 international bestsellers certified and acknowledged by amazon.com.

Maximillien de Lafayette is one of the world's leading linguists and authorities on the culture, civilization and legal systems of the Arab World, Islam, and the Middle East.

After the collapse of the regime of Saddam Hussein, President George Bush and The White House most brilliant political and legal minds decided to write a New Constitution for Iraq.

The White House drafted the first copy of the proposed Constitution, and asked America's most prestigious law school (Yale University, School of Law) to review the document and translate it to Arabic, later on to be submitted to the Iraqi Council, then the governing body of Iraq.

Being a scholar, a jurist, a world-renown linguist, and an exceptionally expert in these fields, Yale University School of Law commissioned Maximillien de Lafayette to translate The White House's draft of the new Constitution of Iraq.

The Book "On The Road To Ultimate Knowledge: Extraterrestrial Tao Of The Anunnaki And Ulema" co-authored by Dr. Ilil Arbel retraces Maximillien's spiritual and metaphysical biography, and passages from his life with the Enlightened Masters and Ascended Anunnaki-Ulema in the East and Europe.
Available at amazon.com

*** *** ***

Books by Maximillien de Lafayette
You might consider

Author's website:
http://www.maximilliendelafayettebibliography.org/biblio
Author's book on spirituality, mediumship, healing, remote
viewing, psychic abilities and supernatural powers.
Contact: delafayette6@aol.com

Maximillien de Lafayette
AMERICA's & WORLD's BEST
PSYCHICS & HEALERS WHO CARE MOST
ABOUT YOU
Names, Profiles, Services, Rates & Contact

Hall of Fame of the Most Caring
Lightworkers

Calendar of Hours & Days Which Bring You Bad Luck & Good Luck: How to Positively Change your Future

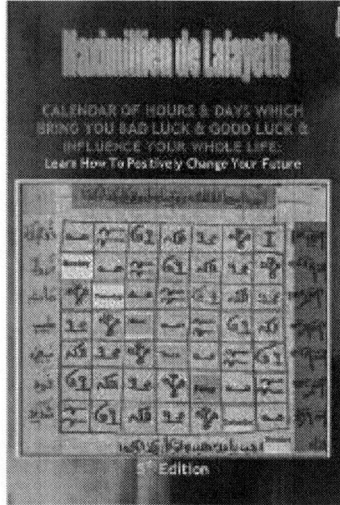

What is luck?

Merriam-Webster's definition of "Luck":

a- A force that brings good fortune or adversity.

b- The events or circumstances that operate for or against an individual.

But what is that "force" that brings good fortune or adversity? And how events or circumstances "operate" for or against an individual? Merriam-Webster does not provide an explanation.

There is a force that shapes and conditions luck; it is the force of the Maktoob, meaning what it is already written in the "Kitbu Dounia", meaning the book of our life, the book of our fate; the book of our destiny.

And how do we explain the mode of operation of events or circumstances that work for us or against us?

The mode of operation of what constitutes "Luck" is always conditioned by unseen metaphysical factors, only known to the Anunnaki Ulema and Sahiriin.

Basically, these factors include:

Factors which influence your future and luck:

• Maktoob.

194

The fluctuation of the "Grid of Calendar" of the good hours and bad hours in our lives: Rizmanah. The calendar of hours and days of your life which bring you good luck and bad luck.
• Some hours are positive, others negative.

Kharta-Makan, which means your zone. In other words, where you live; the location of your home, office, and other places you have lived at and/or you shall occupy in the future.

Ismu, which means your name. It is very true that your name plays a paramount role on the landscape of your luck, future, success and failures.

In summary, time, places and even your name are part of the scenario of the film of your life on the screen of your existence on Earth, and beyond. The Enlightened Masters don't believe in coincidence (s). They have told us that everything in our lives happened for a reason. There are reasons we fully understand as the consequences of our deeds, acts and decisions. And there are reasons we don't understand. Are they caused by others?Are they dictated by fate? Can we change the results, outcome and consequences of these reasons, and alter their effect on our lives, success, happiness, and failure? Yes, we can to a certain degree. This book will show you how!

The book includes:
* Factors which influence your future and luck
* The influence of the Anunnaki's programming of our brain and fate: A rare lecture on luck
* How to read Shashat; the screen of the unknown
* Rizmanah; Discover the calendar of your bad luck and good luck
* Learn how to remove your bad luck
* Learn how to create a good luck
* Daily chart/calendar of your good hours and bad hours in your life
* What to do and not to do during these hours and these days
* Best hours and best days, worst hours and worst days for
* Employees
* Booksellers
* Writers
* Investment
* Real estate business
* looking for a new apartment
* Buying gold

* Buying hard currency
* Selling your art
* Asking for raise and promotion
* Stocks and Shares (trade, selling or buying)
* For writing/submitting proposals and grants
* Job applications
* Meeting new people
* Selling new ideas
* Opening a new business
* Signing contracts, etc...
* Importance of your name in shaping good luck
* Writing/equating your name in Ana'kh Phoenician
* How to write/transpose your name in the Sahiriin language
* Map of United States lucky and unlucky zones
* Case Study: Unhealthy energy and vibrations that damage you and negatively affect your future
* Esoteric techniques you could use to positively influence or improve your future and business by protecting yourself against evildoers
* Grid useful for business, negotiations, meetings
* Foreseeing your future is not enough. You must protect yourself as well. Learn how to do it.
* Grid "Ain Ali" to be used to prevent others from hurting you
* Going back in time and creating a brighter future.

*** *** ***

Psychics-Mediums' Spirits Séances and Witchcraft. ROSTER OF SPIRITS, ANGELS AND DEMONS AND HOW TO COMMUNICATE WITH THEM

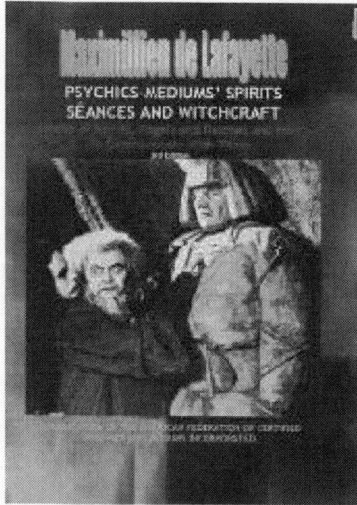

Before you start to do anything or formulate any idea, you should keep in mind three important things:

• a-Spirits, entities, and presences have numerous names, classes and categories, such as the:
• Gaffarim
• Ezraelim
• Ezrai-il
• Afrit
• Ghool
• Ghoolim
• Djinn "Jinn"
• Gallas
• So on...

Each class and each category has its own pre-requisites and protocol.
• b-Deceased people are sometimes called spirits; the spirits of dead people. Many mediums, channelers and psychics claim to be in touch with the spirits. Nonsense! Nobody on Earth can reach the dead, except during the 40 day period, following

their death. And very few people in the entire universe can communicate with dead people, if some criteria are met, and the dead ones are still trapped in Marsha (The doomed zone).

• c-Dead people are not part of the roster of spirits and entities, but are included as "Departed Ones". The book explains step-by-step how to communicate with them.

II. What is the doomed zone (Marsha)?

The doomed zone is a dimension very close to Earth. Basically, it is a location where dead people are confused and trapped in time and space, because of many reasons, such as:

• a-They died from a brutal act, which could be an accident, a murder, a homicide, a suicide, hanging, so on.

• b-They do not fully realize that they are dead.

• c-They are still attached to physical desires, objects, places, and people (Relatives, siblings, parents, friends) they loved so much before they passed away.

• d-They are asking for justice, and in many instances, seeking revenge. So on...

Thus, in their state of mind, death is something they can't either understand or cope with. And as long as, they feel that way, they are doomed, and will remain trapped in that dimension. They need help. Somebody here on Earth, or in that dimension must explain to them that they are dead, and that it is time to move on.These trapped people can be contacted only during the 40 day period previously mentioned. Nevertheless, the Sahiriin could communicate with them, even after the 40 day period has expired, assuming that they have not yet left the doomed zone. Some, stay there for hundreds of years. And this is why we call their zone, the doomed zone.

III. Khirbat-infar zone: Adjacent to Marsha, there is another macabre doomed zone, called Khirbat-infar, where souls and spirits of dead people were/are trapped for centuries, and remained unable to free themselves because of their deeds and actions. The Sahiriin told us that the perturbed Nafash (Soul) of many famous historical figures are trapped in the Khirbat-infar doomed zone. These doomed spirits are of no help to us. And contacting them or summoning them is useless, claim the Sahiriin.

IV. Roster of spirits and entities:

a-70,000 entities:

The book of the Sahiriin listed approximately 70,000 entities, encompassing demons, angels, afarit, djinns, beasts, unidentified bio-organic creatures, ghoolim, ezraelim, ghouls, so on. There is no need to remember all the names of these entities. It would not serve any purpose. Instead, we should learn the names of those entities, who according to the Sahiriin, were/are willing to respond to our summons and Talabaat (Requests). The Sahiriin call them the Moustajabiin.

This book will show you step-by-step how to communicate with all those entities, and provides you with a roster of Spirits, Angels and Demons and Multidimensional Entities you can call upon if you master the techniques of the initiated adepts....all are here in this fascinating book.

Encyclopedic Dictionary of Spirits' Languages and Lightworkers' Terminology and Secrets you Never Knew

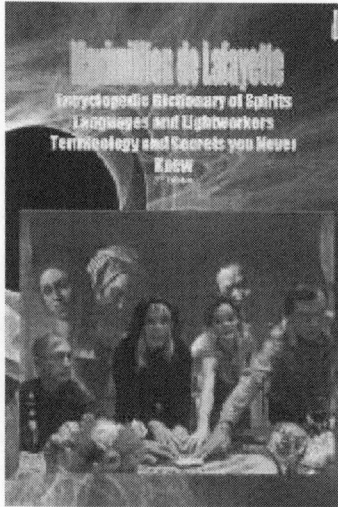

On the cover: The first lady of the occult and supernatural, Patti Negri, conducting a spirits' séance. Official Handbook of the American Federation of Certified Psychics-Mediums Incorporated. Paperback book available at www.lulu.com.

The world's first glossary/terminology and explanation of concepts and ideology in Loughaat (Spirits and Lightworkers' Languages) and English. The secret 16 languages used by the Spirits, Sahiriin, Tahiriin, Mounawariin, Allamah, Djinns, Afarit,

Ghouls, Angels, Demons, Ghosts, Noble Eastern Lightworkers Mediums, Psychics and Channelers and Mystic Ulema.

This unique book is the comprehensive Glossary/Terminology and Explanation of Concepts and Ideology in Loughaat and English. Used by the Spirits, Sahiriin, Tahiriin, Mounawariin, and Mystic Anunnaki Ulema.

Almost 90% of the words, expressions and sentences found in this glossary and vocabulary are commonly, frequently and jointly used by all spirits and entities, including angels and demons.

However, very particular words, phrases, Istijabaat, Talaabat and commands are precisely and exclusively used by certain classes and categories of spirits and entities. Those who are familiar with dead languages and languages of the ancient world of the Middle East, Near East and Anatolia will immediately notice that many words in the spirits and entities languages are frequently found in various languages and scriptures of the ancient world, such as Akkadian, Sumerian, Assyrian, Old Babylonian, Ugaritic, Phoenician, Ana'kh (The Anunnaki's language), even in Aramaic, Hebrew and Arabic.

Languages of the spirits and lightworkers:

• a-The entities who belong to the "Higher or Superior Spirits" have a dignified language. They communicate with us in a very precise and clear manner. They are truthful, humble and friendly.

• b-The entities who belong to the "Lower or Inferior Spirits" are usually arrogant, deceitful, and communicate with us in a vulgar and aggressive manner. They love to play tricks on us, and quite often they give us wrong information.

• c-Those who are trapped in the doomed zone are angry, confused, and vengeful. Consequently, their language is aggressive and confusing.

• d-The noble spirits of antiquity speak in Ana'kh, and/or in an ancient language from the Middle/Near East. They are called "Arwaah Karima", meaning the noble spirits.

• e-The afrit and djinns have their own language; they use macabre and dark expressions. It is almost impossible to understand what they are saying.

• f-The spirits of the Anunnaki Ulema speak in every known language on Earth.

Note: The spirits also use short sentences in answering Taaleb's questions and requests. And in many instances, they answer by yes or no.

In certain cases, they reply by moving objects in different directions, depending on the demands, requests and commands of the Taaleb; this happens, when the spirits and entities do not manifest themselves physically.

Some of the 16 languages of lightworkers, entities, spirits, and angels:

• Nouriin: The language of the angels
• Malaa-iikiyah: Another word for the language of the angels. Malaa-iikiyah derived from Malaak, which means angel in many ancient languages, including Hebrew, Aramaic, Urdu, Farsi, Turkish and Arabic
• Fasida: The language of entities of the Lower Sphere
• Tahira: The language of spirits from the Higher Sphere
• Charrir: The language of evil spirits
• Iblisi: The language of the "devil"
• Rouhaniya: The language of the Spiritualists of the Middle East and the Near East.
• Nouraniya: The Mounawariin language.
• Ana'kh: The language of the Anunnaki Ulema.
• Fikraya: Telepathic language used by both the Enlightened Masters and non-physical presences
• Sawda: The language of the Afrit, Djinns and Ghools

21st Edition. THE EXTRATERRESTRIAL BOOK OF RAMADOSH: 13 Anunnaki Ulema Techniques To Live Longer, Happier, Healthier, Wealthier

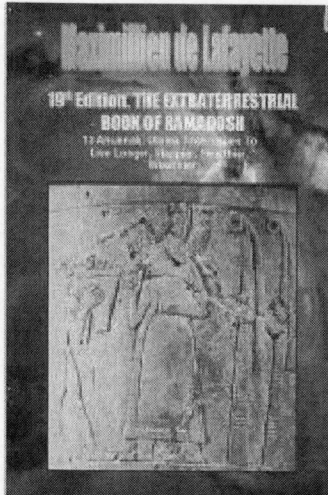

The "Book of Ramnadosh" is the ULTIMATE Book of Eastern Mediums, Psychics and Ascended Masters. You will never ever find these Anunnaki Ulema techniques in any other book. They are herewith presented for the first time in history by Maximillien de Lafayette. No religion, no esoteric teachnings and no other spiritual master (s) have ever discussed or taught the techniques and lessons of Ramadosh. The "Book of Ramadosh" is possibly the greatest book on the power of mind, supernatural, occult, Anunnaki-Ulema extraordinary powers, and how to acquire and develop extraordinary paranormal powers, ever published in the West.
Learn their techniques that will change your life for ever.
You will never be the same person again. This book reveals knowledge that is thousands of years old. Generally, such a statement would bring to mind images of the occult, hidden mysteries, perhaps ancient religious manuscripts. But the Book of Ramadosh is different. It is based on "Transmission of Mind", used eons ago by the Anunnaki and their remnants on Earth. Written by Maximillien de Lafayette, author of 250 books on the Anunnaki, and the world leading authority on Anunnaki/Ulema. The book not only gives you techniques that could bring you health, happiness, and prosperity, but goes deeply into the why and how these techniques do so. Learn how to revisit past/future & travel in time/space; see dead friends & pets in afterlife; secret hour to open Conduit & zoom into your Double & multiple universes; bring luck & change your future.

It includes:
Godabaari Technique:Technique/practice aimed at developing a faculty capable of making objects move at distance by using your mind
• Developing the Conduit
• Moving objects by using mental powers
Gomari Technique
• The exercise
• The equipment
• The technique
Gomatirach-minzari Technique: The Minzar technique: Known as the "Mirror to Alternate Realities"
• Creating your own world
• The Minzar technique

Gubada-Ari Technique: How to find the healthiest spots and luckiest areas on earth, including private places and countries, and take advantage of this
• The Triangle of Life technique
• Synopsis of the theory
• Materials
• IThe technique
Cadari-Rou'yaa Technique: The technique that develop the faculty of reading others' thoughts, intentions, and feelings. Cadari-Rou'yaa is also a method to diagnose health, and prevent health problems from occurring in the present, and in the future.
Chabariduri Technique: Technique/exercise to develop the faculty of remote viewing.
Daemat-Afnah Technique
• Technique/exercise for how to stay and look 37 permanently
• Understanding human life-span and our body longevity
• The brain motor
• Vibrations, frequencies, and luck in life
• The Conduit: Health/youth/longevity
Da-Irat Technique: This technique eliminates stress, through one's self-energy. In other words, it is an Ulema technique used to energize one's mind and body, and to eliminate worries that are preventing a person from functioning properly everywhere, including office, school, home, hospital, social gatherings, etc.
Dudurisar Technique: The ability to rethink and examine past events in your life, change them, and in doing so, you create for yourself a new life and new opportunities. To a certain degree, and in a sense, it is like revisiting your past, and changing unpleasant events, decisions, choices, and related matters that put you where you are today.
Arawadi Technique: Technique to develop a supernatural power or faculty that allows initiated ones to halt or send away difficulties, problems and mishaps into another time and another place, thus freeing themselves from worries, anxiety and fear
Baaniradu Technique: The healing touch technique.
Bari-du Technique: The technique that allows you to zoom into an astral body or a Double.

203

United States National Register of Tested, Certified and Bona Fide Lightworkers, Psychics and Mediums (THE WORLD'S BEST PSYCHICS AND MEDIUMS)

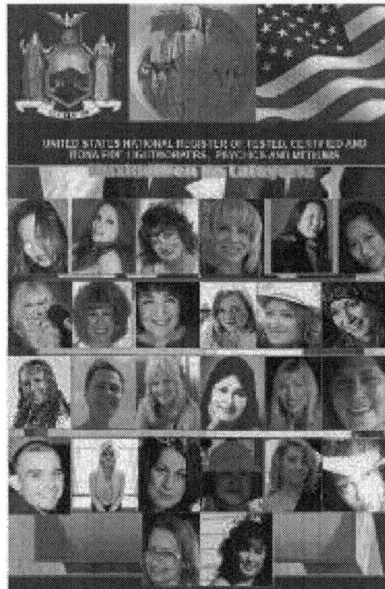

How to Learn the Languages of the Spirits, Ghosts, Angels, Afrit, Djinns, Demons and Entities and Converse with Them

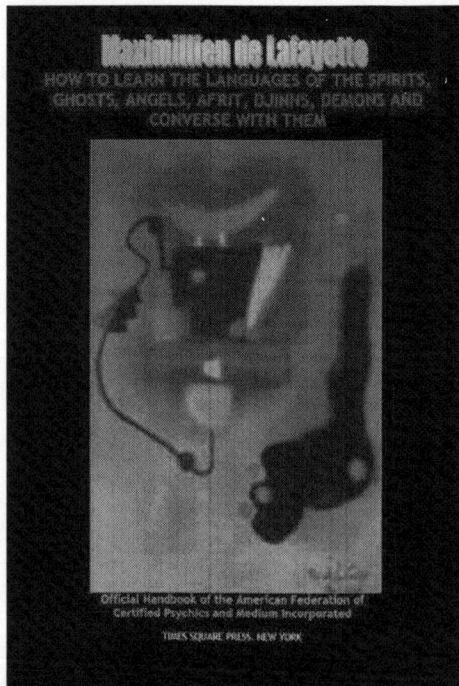

This series covers all the aspects and facets of the languages, vocabulary, words, sentences, conversations, commands, spells, glossary and terminology of the Spirits, Angels, Afarit, Djinns, Demons and Eastern Enlightened Masters and Noble Lightworkers. It teaches you step-by-step how to converse with them in their primordial languages.
From the contents:

* The TV paranormal and ghosts shows' farce
* Languages to be used in various spiritual and metaphysical communications
* Glossary/Terminology and explanation of concepts and ideology in spirits' languages (Loughaat) and English
* The 16 languages of entities, spirits, and angels
* How to converse with angels, demons, Afarit, Djinns, spirits and entities
* In what language, Angels talk to psychics-mediums?
* Angels' communications, angelic messages, technology and recording devices
* The mind, holographic energy and vibrations
* Angelic messages conveyed via pictures
* Comments and explanations of psychics-mediums: Brian Hunter, Justin Chase Mullins, Tina Saelee, Eugenia Macer-Story, Shannon Leischner, Reverend Christa Urban, Suzanne Grace, Patti Negri, Daved Beck, Dr. Linda Salvin, Shellee Hale, Pam Coronado
* Conversing with the "Primordial Angels" (The earliest and first angels in heaven and on Earth) and the "Later Angels"
* The concept and origin of angels
* Language of the "Primordial Angels" and the "Later Angels"
* Roster of Angels known to have interacted with humans and summoned by Sahiriin, Mounawariin, Eastern lightworkers (Psychics, mediums) and Taaleb
* Most Notable "Primordial Fallen Angels"
* Most Notable Fallen Angels in Judeo-Christian-Islamic scriptures
* Gallery of Primordial Angels
* Phoenician Pre-Biblical Angels
* Pre-Biblical Canaannite Angels
* Egyptian Pre-Biblical Angels
* Mesopotamian Pre-Biblical Angels
* Sargonic Pre-Bible Angels
* Sumero-Akkadian Primodial Angels, Pre-Biblical Angels

* Mayan Pre-Biblical Angels
* Roman Pre-Biblical Angels
* How to talk to Afarit and Djinns
* Roster of destructive and dangerous Demons-Afarit you should never summon
* How to talk to ghosts "Ashbaah"
* Roster of spirits and entities
* What is the doomed zone?
* The most practical way to summon an entity
* Roster of "Later Angels" you can summon
* The bad hours and the good hours for summoning entities and spirits
* The d ifferent kinds of spirits and entities' apparitions
* Gallery of ghosts/spirits/orbs photos: The fake and the real
* The most powerful Talabaat, Istijabaat, commands and spells
* Exercises on conversing with a spirit
* Lightworkers recommended by the author

How to Become an Enlightened Psychic, Medium and Metaphysical Master: Handbook of Curriculum, Lessons, Training, Supernatural Techniques and Powers

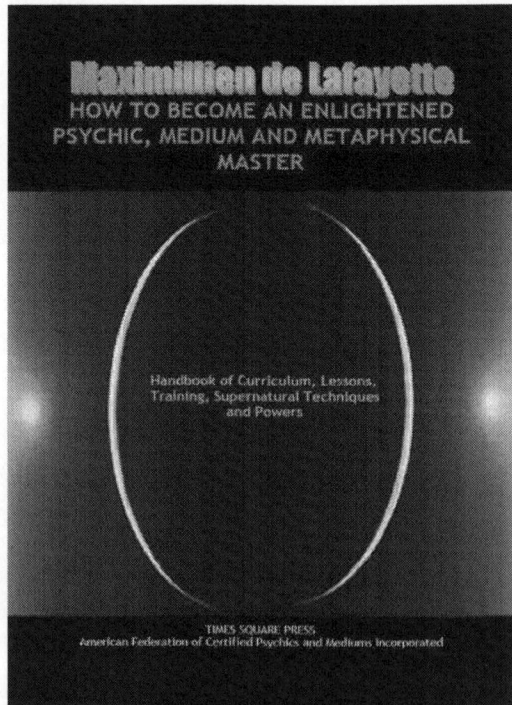

Maximillien de Lafayette
HOW TO BECOME AN ENLIGHTENED PSYCHIC, MEDIUM AND METAPHYSICAL MASTER

Handbook of Curriculum, Lessons, Training, Supernatural Techniques and Powers

TIMES SQUARE PRESS
American Federation of Certified Psychics and Mediums Incorporated

The book includes:
- How to become a perfect psychic
- How to become a perfect medium
- How to become a perfect healer
- How to become expert in remote viewing and locating missing persons
- How to find the healthiest spots and luckiest areas on Earth, and take advantage of it!
- Foreseeing the future and rewinding time
- Esoteric techniques that allows initiated ones to halt or send away problems and mishaps to another time and another place
- How to enter that parallel dimension and leave there all your troubles
- How to Use Your Mind Power to do the Impossible
- How to Read Peoples' Vibes and Thoughts, and Know Who They Really Are Just by Looking at Them (See their Aura, Sense their Vibes, Feel their Energy
- How to read Shashat; the screen of the unknown Rizmanah; Discover the calendar of your bad luck and good luck
Learn how to remove your bad luck
Learn how to create a good luck
Daily chart/calendar of your good hours and bad hours in your life
What to do and not to do during these hours and these days
- Importance of your name in shaping good luck
- Esoteric techniques you could use to positively influence or improve your future and business by protecting yourself against evildoers
- Instructions and Techniques for Commanding Spirits and Communicating with Angels and Entities
- Learn how to talk to entities, spirits, souls, presences
Learn how to befriend spirits.
Learn how to set-up a spirits séance
- Magical writing against powerful people who could be a threat to you
- Practical and simplified techniques to create a mediumship séance and communicate with the dead, spirits, angels, demons, departed pets, and entities from the after-life
- Magical Talismans To Succeed In Life, Protect Yourself From Others And Summon Spirits
- Ulema Techniques and Tarot Deck to See Your Future. (The world's most powerful secret techniques for foreseeing your

future on Earth and in other dimensions
• 13 Anunnaki Ulema Techniques To Live Longer, Happier, Healthier, Wealthier
• Ulema Baaniradu: How to Acquire a Healing Touch
• How to Move Objects at Distance Using Your Mind

This book is unique and extremely useful for many reasons. Mainly because it provides both the beginner and experienced practitioner with the necessary guidance, training, methods and techniques to communicate with various kinds and categories of entities, to foresee future events, and above all how to effectively develop extraordinary supernatural powers.

How to Become an Enlightened Tarot Psychic Reader and Foresee the Future

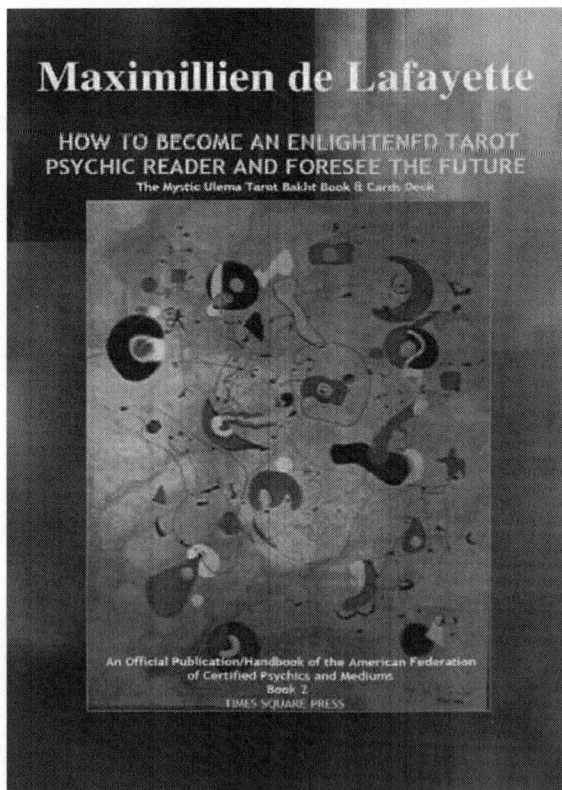

It includes:
* 1-How to foresee your future in this dimension and beyond.
* 2-The importance of your name and its link to the future.
3-How to create your magical tarot table and read the cards.
* 4-Complete set of your personalized Tarot Cards Deck.
5-How to use the secret Ulema Warka Cards to bring you good fortune and succeed in life.

This is the most powerful and effective esoteric Tarot book ever published in the West.
Author's website: maximilliendelafayettebibliography.com

From the publishers: This series of 3 volumes (Approximately 900 pages plus numerous charts) was produced as an extensive handbook and a curriculum to be used by professional psychics, mediums, healers, seers, and lightworkers.
It is based upon the 250 books previously written in the fields of supernatural and paranormal by the Mystic Ulema, Maximillien de Lafayette.
The series should not be considered as a "repetitious" or a "recycling work" from his previous published books and encyclopedias. To many readers, de Lafayette's work is overwhelming.
Consequently, many topics and important subjects in these fields were lost in the immensity of information, lectures and findings provided in his massive published work.
De Lafayette's work is too much, too large, and too varied; this has created some inconvenience and difficulties in finding the subjects and topics of interest to many readers, simply because they were scattered on hundreds of thousands of pages which appeared under hundreds of titles.
You do admit, that it is a hard task to find particular subjects you are interested in, without going through the entire published work of the author.
This fact has convinced us that -in the best interest of the readers and practitioners- we should provide the professional lightworkers with a concise set that leads them directly to the area (s) of their interest, and which is

closely related to their practice.
This set serves these purposes.

This series of three books will show you and teach you how
to become an effective and enlightened medium, psychic
and metaphysical healer.
It will also provide you with lessons, practical training, and
step-by-step instructions on how to find, learn, develop
and use esoteric techniques which produce astonishing
supernatural and paranormal results; techniques and
know-how which were shrouded in secrecy for thousands
of years, such as:
* 1-How to effectively communicate with entities, spirits
and the dead in general.
* 2-How to set up your séances.
* 3-How to summon and command spirits, entities and
elements from different dimensions.
* 4-Remote viewing.
* 5-How to locate missing people.
* 6-How to develop your Supersymetric Mind.
* 7-How to enter multiple dimensions, such as non-
physical dimensions, an adjacent dimension, a parallel
dimension.
* 8-How to foresee future events.
* 9-How to see the Aura.
* 10-How to visit the past and the future.
* 11-How to read others' mind.
* 11-Witchcraft, psychic, mediumship, and paranormal
ultimate techniques.
All are based upon the Kira'at (Readings) and Dirasaat
(Study) of the Enlightened Masters Ulema.

The present book (Volume II) introduces and outlines
some of the major topics and exercises, the seeker of
enlightenment learns in the first two years at the Mystic
Ulema Ma'ahad. The actual curriculum is much extensive
and complicated. Nevertheless, I have selected for you,
important concepts, techniques, and Dirasaat that the
Western mind could understand to a certain degree.

How To Become An Effective Energy Healer And Master Of The Healing Touch: Handbook of Curriculum, Lessons, Training, Supernatural Techniques and Powers

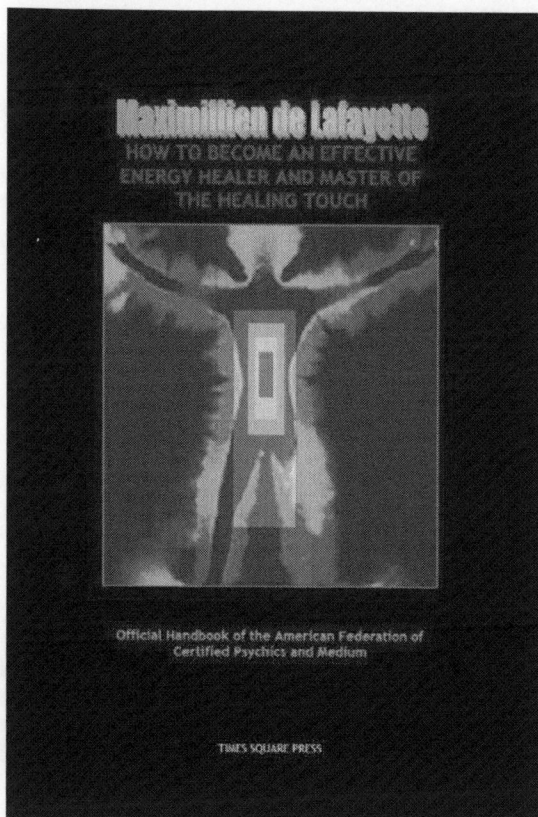

This book will show you and teach you how to become an effective and accomplished energy healer, and provide you with lessons, practical training, and step-by-step instructions on how to use the Healing Touch, find, learn, develop esoteric Energy Healing techniques which produce astonishing supernatural and paranormal results; techniques and know-how which were shrouded in secrecy for thousands of years; they are herewith introduced to the readers and the lightworkers as part of the curriculum and training/orientation programs of the American Federation of Certified Psychics and

211

Mediums.

The present work deals with energy healing and not faith healing, for faith healing belongs to strong religious beliefs, angels' interaction and a multitude of factors which don't fit in the scenario of scientific and metaphysical healing, and don't relate to the contents of this book.

Thus, the study, exploration, training, and techniques as presented in this book pertain exclusively to bio-organic, mental-physical, and the extra-dimensional energy, emanated from the human body and the human mind, which can be revealed and detected in the laboratory, as well as in the immediate physical effects on the physical body, and our environment.

To become an effective energy healer, the practitioner must fully understand:
• 1-The nature of energy. In other words, what is energy? And how it works?
• 2-Sources and levels of energy.
• 3-How does energy (Bad or good) affect the mind and the body?
• 4-Techniques for animating and activating the practitioner's energy.
• 5-How does energy appear to those who can see it?
• 6-The meaning of colors of energy.
• 6- How to block negative vibes.
• 7- How to stop attracting negative people to your life.
• 8- How to discover the energy of the mind and the body
• 9- How to find energy's good days and bad days, and
• energy's good hours and the bad hours.
• 10- Ousoul; the universe's rules and the rhythm of the Micro Wheel and Macro Wheel.
• 11-How to reverse the flux of bad energy, bad days, and bad hours.
• 12- Mintaka Difaya: Protecting your zone.
• 13- The healing touch technique and mechanism, including the prerequisites and preparation.

The present work answers all those questions, and provides pragmatic techniques which enable the lightworker and practitioner to become an effective energy healer and master of the healing touch.

How to Become an Enlightened Psychic Detective and Remote Viewer: Ulema Psychometry Lessons, Training & Techniques to locate Missing People and Identifying Places & Objects.

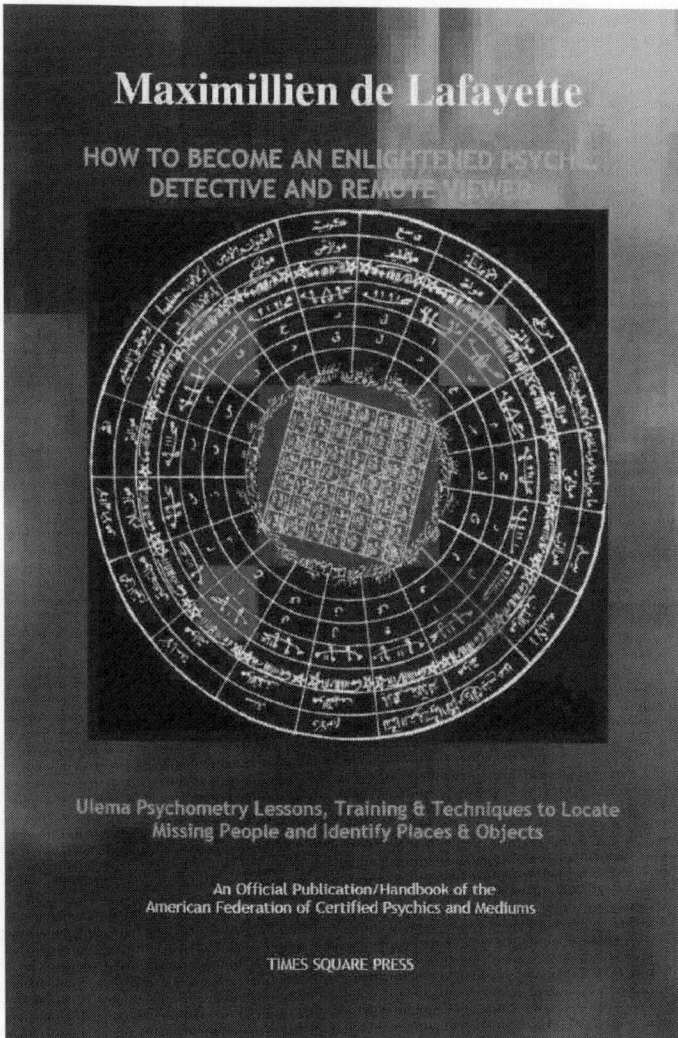

Maximillien de Lafayette

HOW TO BECOME AN ENLIGHTENED PSYCHIC
DETECTIVE AND REMOTE VIEWER

Ulema Psychometry Lessons, Training & Techniques to Locate
Missing People and Identify Places & Objects

An Official Publication/Handbook of the
American Federation of Certified Psychics and Mediums

TIMES SQUARE PRESS

It includes:
* 1-Techniques for reading the thoughts, intentions and feelings of others;

* 2-Learning from sensing the vibrations of objects and people at distance;
* 3-How to develop remote viewing capabilities; how to identify and locate hidden objects;
* 4-How to find missing persons anywhere in the world;
* 5-Exercises for testing and enhancing the master and the students' levels of learning and implementing these fabulous and mot secret esoteric and supernatural faculties and powers.

This series of psychics, mediums & healers handbook of curriculum, lessons, training and techniques, was produced as an extensive handbook & a curriculum to be used by professional psychics, mediums, healers, seers & lightworkers. It is based upon the 250 books previously written in the fields of supernatural and paranormal by the Mystic Ulema, Maximillien de Lafayette. The series should not be considered as a "repetitious" or a "recycling work" from his previous published books and encyclopedias. To many readers, de Lafayette's work is overwhelming. Consequently, many topics and important subjects in these fields were lost in the immensity of information, lectures and findings provided in his massive published work.

De Lafayette's work is too much, too large, and too varied; this has created some inconvenience and difficulties in finding the subjects and topics of interest to many readers, simply because they were scattered on hundreds of thousands of pages which appeared under hundreds of titles. You do admit, it is a hard task to find particular subjects you are interested in, without going through the entire published work of the author.

This fact has convinced us that -in the best interest of the readers and practitioners- we should provide the professional lightworkers with a concise set that leads them directly to the area (s) of their interest, and which is closely related to their practice. This set serves these purposes.

The present book introduces and outlines some of the major topics and exercises of Cadari-Rou'yaa, Chabariduri, & Fik'r-Telemetry, (called psychometry in the Western world) the seeker of enlightenment learns in the third & fourth years at the Ulema Ma'ahad. The actual curriculum is much extensive and complicated.

Nevertheless, we have selected for you, important concepts, Kira'at and Dirasaat that the Western mind could understand to a certain degree.

The techniques, methods, art and science of remote viewing, locating and finding objects and missing persons, gathering information about people, objects & places just by looking at photographs of objects, people and places &by sensing the vibrations emanated from photographs and objects, and in many instances by touching objects and photographs, are grouped into the Mystic Ulema Ilmu (Learning) under 3 secret esoteric techniques known as:

* 1-Cadari-Rou'yaa
* 2-Chabariduri
* 3-Fik'r-Telemetry, called psychometry in the Western world.

These techniques were shrouded in secrecy for almost 5,000 years. They were developed by the Mystic Anunnaki Ulema Jamiya in the Near East, and some 3,000 years ago, the priests of Ra and Melkart began to implement them in Egypt, Sumeria and Phoenicia.

The Babylonian & the Chaldeans were famous for their practice of these esoteric techniques, and some of the techniques and exercises were explained at length in the Book of Ramadosh. Cadari-Rou'yaa, Chabariduri &Fik'r were discussed in depth in several previous published work of Maximillien de Lafayette. They are herewith introduced to the readers & lightworkers as part of the curriculum and training programs of the American Federation of Certified Psychics & Mediums

*** *** ***

215

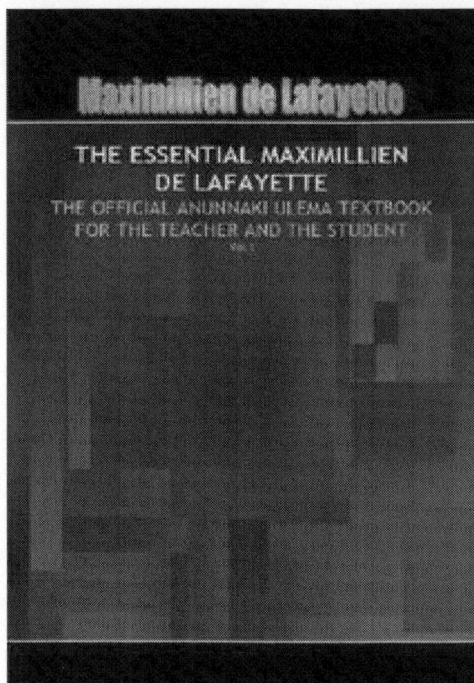

THE ESSENTIAL MAXIMILLIEN DE LAFAYETTE: The Official Anunnaki Ulema Textbook for the Teacher and the Student. In 2 Volumes

THE ESSENTIAL MAXIMILLIEN DE LAFAYETTE is a synopsis of the 200 books, the author wrote on the subjects of the Anunnaki, the afterlife, the supernatural powers of the Anunnaki Ulema, the paranormal, the occult, parallel dimensions, multiple universes, the Conduit, the Supersymetric Mind, the Double, the Astral Body, communications with spirits and entities from the world beyond, the power of the mind, mediumship, channeling, the enlightenment, the Fourth Dimension, the Fifth Dimension, Earth energy, healing, the world outside time and space, extraterrestrials, time-travel, reading the future, and similar topics. This is NOT a repetitious book. It was intentionally compiled from the most important concepts, theories, esoteric techniques, wisdom, Eastern philosophy, the world of the mystic seers "The Ulema", and particularly the teaching of Maximillien de Lafayette.

This series consists of 2 massive volumes, each exceeding 700 pages (50 MB). This manual is also the Official Anunnaki Ulema Textbook for the Teacher and the Student. De Lafayette wrote more than 800 books, 200 of them are in these fields. Consequently, it is quasi-impossible for the reader to purchase all these books. The present work contains knowledge, techniques and revelations, no other author has ever discussed, simply because they emerge from the teachings of the author's Enlightened Masters and his own philosophy. Add to the fact, that no other author or researcher has ever approached these topics, simply because they were brought to the West, for the first time in history, from the author's own vision and perspective. You will NOT find the material of this book in any other work, and/or in any library. As a matter of fact, the material of the present work (Volumes 1 and 2) is to a certain degree in sharp contrast with what it has been said or written in these fields. No one can claim that this book was inspired by or based upon any existing published book. It is a journey to new dimensions, and analysis of the physical and mental worlds as interpreted personally by the author.

The contents include:1. Description of the Afterlife in all its states and dimensions. 2. What do we see when we enter the afterlife zone? 3. The various states of metamorphosis of the mind-body of a deceased person in the after-life. 4. Experiences dead people encounter in the next dimension. 5. How to bring good luck to your endeavors and surmount obstacles and hardship that prevent you from succeeding in life. 6. How to use Earth energy to your advantage and block others' bad vibes and vicious intentions that are causing you harm and damage. 7. The first stage of the afterlife during the 40 day period following death, and how to communicate with your departed loved ones and pets. 8. How the Anunnaki created us genetically 65,000 years ago. 9. The mysterious and hidden world of the Anunnaki Ulema as the author knew it and explored it. 10. Foreseeing the future and rewinding time; revisiting your childhood and past life in different dimensions. 11. How the Masters, the Mounawiriin, and the Anunnaki Ulema transpose you from the present to the future? 12. How to develop The Supersymetric Mind. 13. Study of the influence of the Anunnaki's programming of our brain and fate. 14. The duplicate image of ourselves or reproduction of our body in other dimensions. 15.

The early human species and races created by the extraterrestrials. 16. How to learn The Anunnaki Ulema supernatural and mind power techniques. 17. Entering a parallel dimension; Is it possible to enter a parallel dimension and leave there all your troubles? YES! 18. Occult techniques and talismans to protect yourself from others. And much much more.-By Dina Vittantonio, Editor.

The United States and the World's Best Psychics, Mediums, Healers, Astrologers, Palmists, Witches and Tarot Readers 2013-2014

Based upon
THE 3rd NATIONAL & INTERNATIONAL ELECTION/VOTE OF THE UNITED STATES AND THE WORLD'S BEST MEDIUMS, PSYCHICS, HEALERS, ASTROLOGERS AND LIGHTWORKERS 2013-2014

Maximillien de Lafayette

OVER 400 PAGES WITH HUNDREDS OF PHOTOS

THE UNITED STATES AND THE WORLD'S BEST PSYCHICS, MEDIUMS, HEALERS, ASTROLOGERS, PALMISTS, WITCHES AND TAROT READERS 2013-2014

Based on the 3rd National/International Vote of the United States & World's Best Lightworkers 2013-2014.

THE WORLD'S #1 REFERENCE & SOURCE OF INFORMATION ON THE MOST POPUPAR & TRUSTED LIGHTWORKERS AROUND THE GLOBE!!

Form for Lightworkers' Nomination for the International/National Vote for the World's Best Psychics, Mediums, Healers, Astrologers and Metaphysical Practitioners
2013-2014

Please keep this form handy. Complete it, update it, revise it constantly and email it to Judith Goldsmith, editor at Stars Illustrated Magazine at newyorkgate@aol.com. Select up to 20 lightworkers in any discipline and area of practice.
Nominations end on December 19, 2014, 1:00 AM, New York Time.

NAMES OF THE NOMINEES

#1 _____

#2 _____

#3 _____

#4 _____

#5 _____

#6 _____

#7 _____

#8 _____

#9 _____

#10_____

#11_____

#12_____

#13_____

#14_____

#15_____

#16_____

#17_____

#18_____

#19_____

#20_____

Remarks/Notes:_____

_____

_____

Form for Filing a Complaint Against a Lightworkers

If you wish to file a complaint against lightworkers in any part of the world, please complete this form and email it to info@americanfederationofcertifiedpsychicsandmediums.org

Your complaint form should contain the following and meet these criteria

1-Nature of the complaint.
2-Name of the lightworker you are filing the complaint against
3-Location of the lightworker (Country, website, his/her phone number, and e-mail.)
4-State your case in detail
5-All claims must be substantiated, no gossip or wild accusations.
6-Date of the incident (s).
7-How much did you pay for the lightworker's services
8-List of witnesses if applicable.
9-State under oath that you are telling the truth (Just email us your notorized statement.)
10-State your full name, address, phone number and the best way and time to contact you.

*** *** ***

NOTES

NOTES

NOTES

Published by
TIMES SQUARE PRESS
New York, Berlin

Printed in the United States of America
2014

Printed in Great Britain
by Amazon.co.uk, Ltd.,
Marston Gate.